ASHES

SINS Series Book 7

EMMA SLATE

Tabula Rasa Publishing

This book is a work of fiction. Names, characters, places, and incidents are the product of the author's imagination or are used fictitiously. Any resemblance to actual events, locales, or persons, living or dead, is coincidental.

Chapter 1
QUINN

My husband gripped my hand and brought it to his lips. His dark eyes were lit with desire and triumph.

I'd said the words to legally bind me to this man. If I hadn't been a coward, I would've clamped my jaw shut and refused to marry him. But I had a healthy dose of self-preservation.

Ori's family surrounded me.

I had no allies.

No weapons.

Nothing—except my memories. They'd come flooding back the moment I'd stepped up onto the altar. Once upon a time, I thought I'd stand next to another man—a blond man. I would've gladly given him the words of my heart. But he'd walked away.

He'd walked away, and now I was married to someone else who stared at me like I was a prize he'd won.

Ori guided me down the aisle, past our guests, his arm wrapped around me.

"You're beautiful," he whispered, his mouth grazing the delicate Italian lace of my veil.

"Thank you," I said. My voice was calm, but my heart thundered in my chest. If only it could gallop away—if only my body could.

"You're no longer upset, are you?" he inquired as he led me toward the house where we'd have our wedding feast.

"Upset?"

"About Camilla?"

Camilla who'd tried to kill me. Camilla and her severed finger. I swallowed down my revulsion and forced myself to lean into his side. "No, I'm not upset. Though I can't say I'm at all pleased with how you chose to protect me." I threw an amused smile at him. I wondered if he could tell it was fake. "I appreciate it, though. The protection, I mean."

Ori threw back his head and laughed. "I told you I would protect you. Actions speak louder than words, don't you agree?"

"Yup." I tried to step away from him, but his grip tightened around me.

"Where are you trying to go?" he demanded. His smile was playful, but his body was taut with tension.

Instinctively, I placed my hand on his chest and looked up at him. I opened my eyes wide and fluttered my eyelashes. "I wanted to change out of the wedding dress and into a party dress," I explained.

He grinned and then his gaze swept down me. "Need some help with those buttons?"

I nearly faltered, thinking about him touching me. But I was Quinn O'Malley, and I knew how to bluster my way through a situation. So, I pressed a kiss along his shaved jaw and said, "I do—but not from you. You, sir, get to wait until tonight before seeing me in my wedding lingerie."

Ori groaned. "Five minutes."

"No," I playfully admonished. "Tonight. When we have the time. Now, we celebrate. Get me a glass of Prosecco."

"Bossy," he murmured, eyes dilating in lust. "I like it."

I forced out a laugh and then ducked out of his arms. I picked up the skirt of my dress and hurried toward the house. When I made it to the door, I waved and then blew him a kiss. I dashed up the stairs, passing the photograph of the three boys, and ducked into the room that had my clothes.

I did need help with all the tiny buttons on the dress, and I'd get one of the maids to help me, but first I needed a moment to gather my thoughts. I went into the bathroom and closed the door. I turned on the faucet, letting the water run. Only then did I finally give into my fear and cry.

Ori had lied to me from the moment I'd woken up in the hospital.

He didn't love me.

We hadn't been planning a life together.

I'd walked out on him.

He'd used my amnesia against me.

I compelled the tears away. I made sure my makeup was perfect, and then I turned off the water. With a deep breath, I opened the door and came face to face with Ori.

He stared at me with fathomless brown eyes.

I tried to bring a smile to my lips, but it wouldn't come.

Ori reached out and took my hands in his and brought my knuckles to his mouth. He kissed one hand and then the other. When I tried to pull back, he tightened his hold.

I didn't like the lurking shadows in his eyes. Dangerous.

"Tell me something, Quinn," he said, tone deceptively mild.

My bones crunched in his strong grip, and I winced in pain.

"When did your memory come back?"

Chapter 2
QUINN

"My memory didn't come back," I lied.

"Quinn, Quinn, Quinn," he taunted. "Do you know one of the things I love most about you? Your inability to hide what you're feeling. Your words say one thing, but your body doesn't lie. You're tense when I touch you. Your smile is slow to come."

He dropped my hands, and I instantly cradled them against my chest.

"So, we can do this the hard way or the easy way. You lie to me again, and you won't like the consequences. And as you know, I'm a man of my word. I follow through." His dark eyes pinned me like an insect to a board. "Answer the question."

"After I said my vows," I admitted. My voice sounded small, weak. Ineffectual. "It all came back."

He inhaled slowly. "Turn around."

I swallowed and for a brief moment, I thought about disobeying, but this was a man I didn't recognize. Gone was the playful lover, the seducer. He'd gotten what he'd wanted, his ring on my finger. We were legally bound. He could hurt me. He *would* hurt me. I'd once been with Sasha. For some reason, he hated that.

Now was not the time to go head-to-head with him, so I turned.

I expected him to rip the dress from my body. To tear away the lace panties I wore and to sink himself inside of me. He was a monster; he'd be playing into the role.

But Ori surprised me when he gently began undoing the buttons of my dress. And then he spoke. "Now that you have your memories back, I don't need to watch what I say. I haven't been completely honest with you, Quinn."

I held in a snort. That was putting it mildly. I placed my hand on the doorframe of the bathroom as he continued undressing me.

"Abruzzo is my middle name, not my last. Do you know what that means?"

I shook my head.

"It means that your last name is not Abruzzo. It's Marino."

"Marino?" I whispered.

I felt him at my back, the heat of him, the strength. He was a brutal man, and he'd been hiding it from me. His lips brushed against my ear when he asked, "Does that name have meaning for you?"

I nodded because I couldn't answer. Words stuck in my throat.

"Your father murdered my oldest brother. Sasha Petrovich took over New York Italian territory. I want it back."

"I'm payment," I said, my tone wooden. "Aren't I?"

Ori's hands reached around to gently cup my breasts as he thrust his erection against my back. "You were, Quinn. I had plans to destroy you. Destroy Sasha Petrovich's woman, destroy Michael O'Malley's daughter. I had plans to break you so thoroughly that I was going to send you back in pieces." One of his hands dropped from my breasts. He wormed his way under the Italian lace skirt, his fingers diving into my panties. His pointer finger rested on the heat of me. If he'd wanted, he could've slid into my body, but he chose to leave his finger there, letting me know that he owned me.

"Why didn't you?" I asked quietly.

His other hand skated down to my hip to haul me back up against him. "Your father died, Petrovich disappeared, and so I changed my course of action. And once I was in your bed, between your legs, I knew I wanted you for myself. I want you round with my child."

Ori's finger gently began to stroke me. Flames of desire erupted under my skin. I tried to stop them, to quell my want for this man, but his hands were magic. It didn't matter that he was a liar and that part of me hated him. He was right—my body did betray me.

"You're mine, Quinn," he grated and then bit my earlobe.

I screamed in pleasure, bowing taut. My release was swift and powerful—and completely out of my control. I collapsed against him.

He whispered soft words of Italian to me as he continued to stroke me.

I closed my eyes and wished I were anywhere else.

Ori gently let me go and stepped back. "Change clothes and then come downstairs. I want to give a toast to my new bride."

Chapter 3
QUINN

I heard the door click shut and breathed out a sigh of relief that I was alone. Leaning over, I took a deep lungful of air as I placed my cheek against the cool wall. I waited for my heartbeat to return to normal, for the flush on my skin to dissipate. Only then did I strip out of my wedding dress. I took the time to hang it up because it was a beautiful gown despite the memories now attached to it. I removed my veil and placed it across the vanity chair.

When I was dressed in another white dress, this one classic yet stylish, I looked in the mirror.

I was married to a Marino.

It was not sinking in.

Fear coated my tongue. Ori Marino was using me in a revenge plot. But Sasha had disappeared over a year ago, so if Ori thought marrying me would draw him out, then he was mistaken.

I shivered when I thought about what Ori had said to me while his finger was inside my body. He'd made me feel expendable. Maybe I still was. I didn't know. He was a

8

Ashes

sociopath. Sociopaths didn't view love and emotion the same as normal people.

He'd played on my weaknesses; I'd been alone and abandoned. He'd given me a picture of a beautiful family. No wonder I'd fallen for him. But clearly Ori didn't love me. I was a prized broodmare.

He would share my bed tonight—and every night thereafter. Bile threatened to climb up my throat, but I choked it down. Ori wouldn't be satisfied until I was pregnant with his child. The child and I would be pawns. Extensions of him.

Desolation threatened to consume me.

There was a wedding feast to attend—and if Ori had to come back up here... He'd never been violent before. Would that change now?

I shoved my feelings aside. There was no time to examine them. I reached for the doorknob of the bedroom when I heard the screams. I rushed down the stairs, nearly tripping in my haste to find the cause. I dashed outside, the smell of smoke on the air. It was pandemonium. Men were throwing their suit jackets onto chairs and running toward the vineyard—the vineyard that was on fire.

Even Ori was in the thick of it, yelling in Italian, obviously directing people.

His grandfather's vineyard was going up in flames—a vineyard that had been in their family for generations. This was their livelihood, their legacy.

And I took complete advantage of the situation. While Ori was distracted, as were most of the guests, I ran back into the house.

I needed to escape.

When I got to the bedroom, I immediately kicked off my heels and threw on a pair of black boots. They didn't have a heel—and I had no way of knowing if they would be comfortable enough to run in, but anything was better than heels. I quickly looked for my purse. I couldn't find it.

Ori must've taken my passport and cell phone.

"Fuck," I cursed.

Well, there was no use worrying about it. I'd have to make a run for it. I couldn't go into the tiny town. The Abruzzos ran the little village.

I had no allies, no money, no ID, no safe haven. But I was leaving anyway and taking my chances. Instead of heading down the front stairs, I took the back. I ducked into the library on the first floor and shut the door. My heart thumped loudly in my ears as I dashed toward the window. I threw it open and stuck my head out. Because it was on the opposite side of the house—away from the vineyard—no one would see me if I slipped away.

I scrambled out the window, feeling an odd sense of déjà vu. It would be nice if my life didn't resort to sneaking out windows trying to escape Ori.

Just as I dropped to the ground, I heard someone coming. I thought about running for the band of trees, but I knew I wouldn't get there in time. I expected to see a man in a suit, one of Ori's men, but I nearly stumbled when I realized it was Camilla.

She was wearing a blush taffeta dress, and her dark hair was twirled up in an elegant bun. Her right hand was bandaged.

"You have a habit of climbing out windows," she remarked. Her tone was mild, but her eyes couldn't conceal her anger.

"Oh, Camilla. Hello," I said with feigned cheer. The woman terrified me. Anyone that could pretend to like me and then drug me with my own medication was not someone I wanted to mess with.

"The wedding feast is on the other side of the house."

"Yes," I said with a nod. "I was just thinking I'd get some fresh air before I joined the party."

"Fresh air? Cut the crap." She took a menacing step toward me. "You were getting ready to make a run for it."

"So what if I was?" I snapped. My temper was on the end of a very frayed rope. "It's none of your business."

"It *is* my business!"

"Why don't you go help put out the fire in the vineyard," I taunted.

"They don't need my help. Ori has it under control. Your friends won't succeed."

"Friends?" I asked, my heart suddenly speeding up. "What friends?"

Camilla rolled her eyes. "I can't imagine why he married you. You're nothing but a dumb bitch!"

She launched herself at me. Even though I was a few inches taller, she was fueled by rage, and she took me down. Before I knew it, I was embroiled in a full-on girl fight. Camilla maneuvered herself on top of me, and she wrapped her hands around my throat. She would've had a better grip except for the bandage.

I went for the injured hand.

She screamed and threw herself off me, giving me time to gulp a deep breath of air. I was ready to take off for the woods—screw the unknown, anything was better than getting my ass kicked by some crazy chick—but as I stood up, Camilla hurled stones at me. Unfortunately, the bitch had a good arm, and she clocked me a few times. My arms took the brunt of it, but one stone managed to hit my shoulder when I ducked at the last moment, trying to protect my head.

The last thing I needed was *another* head injury.

Her energy was limitless. With her pointed aims, she started herding me toward the vineyard—toward the fire.

I had to take Camilla down. She was the only thing standing in my way of escaping. She was insane, unbalanced, and completely delusional. She cursed at me in a mixture of Italian and English.

She grasped a jagged, pale gray stone, weighing it in her hand. If that thing hit its mark, it would do some serious damage.

"What's the matter, pretty girl," she jeered. "Afraid to fight?"

"This isn't a fight; it's an ambush," I threw out. Anything to keep her talking. Anything to give me some time to think.

"He'll thank me, you know. Eventually."

"Plan to take my place?" I smirked. "You do remember he was the one who cut off your finger for trying to kill me. What do you think he'll do this time?"

My words made her pause, but then she started advancing on me again. "You seduced him. He'll give up everything he's working for because of you."

I shook my head. "What are you talking about?"

"Revenge," she spat. "For the deaths of his father and brother. For his best friend."

"His best friend…" I murmured. "You mean Igor?"

"Your *boyfriend* shot him in cold blood. And Ori means to make him pay."

Nausea surged in my belly at Camilla's words. And while I was too busy working through it, she charged me. Even though she was in heels and I was in boots, I still went down.

She aimed the rock for my head and swung. The few hours of training I'd once had with Sasha kicked in. I bucked my body, dislodging Camilla from atop me. The rock missed my head but landed on my shoulder. I immediately picked it up and gripped it in my hand.

And while Camilla was down, I swung with all my force. The rock landed with a sickening crunch to the side of her head. Her eyes rolled back, and her body went limp.

I stood on shaky legs and peered down at her. The yells were diminishing. Maybe they were getting the fire under control. I didn't have much time.

I dropped the rock and ran for the woods.

Chapter 4
SASHA

"Where the fuck is she?" I demanded, adrenaline surging through my body. "How could she not be in her room?"

"Don't fucking yell at me," Barrett growled. "The White Company did their job: they set the vineyard on fire so I could sneak into the house and find Quinn. She wasn't in the room Brandon told us she was in. So if you want to blame anyone, blame Brandon and his shitty Intel."

I raked a hand through my hair—or what was left of it. We were essentially a three-man operation.

A surge of rage made me unbalanced. The bastard had married her, and I hadn't been there in time to stop it. She now shared his last name. I was ready to tear trees out by their roots, but I knew it wouldn't do any good getting distracted.

I'd kill Ori Marino, and then he'd no longer be Quinn's husband.

But I couldn't kill him until we found Quinn and she was safe.

I wanted to charge in, dismantle the house brick by

brick. I was just about to do it when Barrett put her hand on my arm to stop me.

"Hold on," she said. "Brandon's calling." She put her cell phone to her ear. "Yeah? Shit, really? Okay. We're on it. Tie up the loose ends with The White Company and then meet us at the plane." She paused again. "No, we won't leave you behind, Brandon. Shut up or I'll kick your ass the next time I see you." She hung up.

"What happened?" I demanded. My skin felt itchy with the need to move, to do *something*.

"He scouted the area behind the house—he found a body by the library."

"A body?"

"A woman's," she clarified. "Not Quinn, obviously. Brandon saw boot prints heading in the direction of the woods."

I sighed. "Quinn went into the woods?"

"Yup."

"Without a firearm I'm guessing," I muttered. "Not that she'd know how to use it."

"I can take Brandon and find her," Barrett volunteered. "You can stay at the vineyard and…"

"Find Marino?" I shook my head. "Not with his entire family around. Not with all these witnesses. No, I'm going to draw the bastard out—like he's been doing to me. We have to find Quinn before he does."

"Okay." Barrett stuck her phone inside her back pocket. "Let's go."

We started off at a brisk pace, backtracking away from the house. Though it would've been easier to take the direct path to the woods, I was afraid someone would see us.

Part of me thought about slowing down, to give Barrett an easier time, but she didn't complain and kept up.

"You're in good shape," I commented. "Were you ever in this good of shape?"

She snorted as our feet pounded dirt and leaves. "Nope. I was always a runner, though. That comes back pretty easily. But I've been doing a lot of training…you know, to make up for my hip and knee. I'm going to need some monster painkillers when we get to the plane. Then again, I might just settle for Scotch. I like the effects a lot better."

We made it to the main road and then cut up a hill and headed for the trees. I'd done my research of the Abruzzo land and surrounding areas. The thicket wasn't big—only about a mile wide. It still wasn't ideal, trying to find Quinn this way, but she'd been untraceable these last many days. She hadn't been carrying a phone—or if she had been—we hadn't been able to track her that way. Marino had done everything he could to keep her under the radar.

"This is a terrible idea," Barrett said. "How the hell are we supposed to—"

A flock of birds flew over us, the flap of their wings and their calls loud in the otherwise quiet air. I shot Barrett a look and grinned. "Something startled them," I said. "Something that isn't a hunter. My guess? Quinn is that direction."

"You knew that how?" Barrett demanded as she followed me.

"My childhood."

"Are you going to tell me *anything* about that time in your life?"

"It sucked. That's all you need to know about it."

We stopped talking and continued to trek through the woods. I drew my weapon just in case it wasn't Quinn, but a Marino or an Abruzzo, with the same intention of finding Quinn.

The brush of trees cleared away to reveal a flat spot with a few logs and a fire circle. We stopped for a moment to catch our breath. A twig snapped, and I whirled, my Glock raised.

Quinn stumbled into the clearing. Her ankle twisted, and she went down on her hands and knees. And then she let out a long list of curses.

It was the most beautiful sound I'd ever heard.

"Quinn?" Barrett said, taking a step toward her. "Are you okay?"

"No, I'm not okay," Quinn snapped. She raised her head to glare at Barrett, and then her eyes slid to mine. "You're late."

My breath nearly caught in my lungs. "You know who I am?"

Quinn slowly stood up and tested weight on her ankle. She wrinkled her nose when it obviously gave her a twinge of discomfort. "Yeah, you jerk, I know who you are."

I wanted to laugh. Instead, I settled for a smile. "You've got your memory back."

"You knew about my amnesia?"

"Can we play catch up later?" Barrett asked. "These woods are giving me the creeps."

"You and nature," I said, finally unable to hold back my laughter. "We need to get out of here."

I thought about going to Quinn, but I knew if I did, I'd take her into my arms and never let go. And now was not the time or the place to make amends. All I wanted to do was breathe her in.

"Some rescue mission," Quinn drawled. "You couldn't have gotten here an hour ago?"

"Things went a little…awry," Barrett said. She jogged over to Quinn and pulled her into her arms. A moment later, Quinn's arms went around her, but her eyes remained on me.

Barrett whispered something in Quinn's ear I couldn't hear. It had Quinn smiling and nodding. Barrett pulled away and then took Quinn's hand.

"Can you walk okay?" Barrett asked.

"Yes." Quinn took a step forward. I could tell it hurt, but she bit down on her lip and kept going forward.

Barrett looked at me. "Back the way we came?"

I shook my head. "I know a shortcut to the car. This way."

Chapter 5
QUINN

We hiked silently through the woods. Sasha walked in front, I was in the middle, and Barrett brought up the rear. My ankle ached with every step, but I refused to complain. I stared at Sasha's back. It was solid, firm, and even through his shirt, I could tell he was cut. More cut than he'd ever been, maybe.

He felt like a stranger.

And though I was glad they'd both come for me, I wasn't exactly thrilled with having to deal with Sasha.

There were a lot of things between us left unsaid and when we got into it, I knew we'd really get into it.

I didn't know him anymore, and yet I still loved him. Despite that he'd left me. Despite that he was late in rescuing me—the point was, he *had* come for me.

About an hour later, we made it to the car. They'd pulled it off the road and hid it among the bushes.

"Quinn upfront," Sasha commanded.

"Aye, aye," Barrett teased with an irreverent salute. She shot me a wink and gripped my hand tightly in hers. She gave it a squeeze and then let go.

We climbed into the car, and Sasha started the engine. I leaned back against the seat, finally giving in to my exhaustion. The last couple of days had drained me.

A phone vibrated and a moment later, Barrett said, "Brandon got a ride with Angelo. He's safe, and he'll meet us on the tarmac."

"Brandon's here?" I asked. My voice came out a croak. Between Camilla's hands around my neck and not talking for an hour, my throat was sore.

Sasha handed me a bottle of water and then put the car into gear. "Kilmartin came, *da*."

"Who's Angelo?" I unscrewed the lid and took a drink. When I had my fill, I sighed and set the bottle between my legs.

"Leader of The White Company," Sasha finally said.

My eyes widened in surprise when I looked at him— and then I glanced behind me at Barrett. She nodded in confirmation.

"They set the fire?" I guessed.

"Yup," Barrett said. "Please don't ask us anything else about them. We're not at liberty to say."

"We?" I asked.

Sasha cursed in Russian. "Barrett came with me to meet them. I needed back up."

"Why not get your men?" I wondered.

"Too many reasons to list," Sasha said. He maneuvered the car out of the bushes and down the small hill to the main road.

"There are a lot of things we should discuss," Barrett said, "but only once we're Scotland bound."

"I don't want to go to Scotland," I stated, trying to assert what little independence I had. For too long I'd been at the mercy of Ori. I wanted some control back.

"Too bad," Sasha said.

"Idiot," Barrett muttered.

I ignored her. "I have a right to—"

"You married Ori Marino, and that fucker will stop at nothing to get you back. You're not going to Boston where he can find you so easily again. We're going to Scotland where we will discuss how to get you out of this mess. This stupid mess that you got yourself into."

"Big idiot," Barrett voiced.

"Shut up, Barrett!" Sasha growled.

"No, you shut up," I yelled. "You want to know why I'm in this fucking mess to begin with? Because of you, you prick!"

His jaw clenched. "Leaving you was the right thing to do."

"I'm not even talking about that," I snapped, hurt stinging my feelings. "Ori thinks you killed Igor Dolinsky."

Barrett leaned forward and put her head between our shoulders and waited for me to say more.

I slumped down in my seat, suddenly cold. I reached out to open the vents, needing some heat. Sasha turned on the dial, and immediately hot air caressed my fingers.

Pinching the bridge of my nose, I said, "He's after you for so many reasons, Sasha. He wants the New York territory back that you took from the Italians. If I had to guess, I'd say he assumes you killed his father, too."

"The FBI killed Marino Sr.," Sasha said, voice clipped.

"But you and Flynn set him up. Whatever. But I didn't even get the feeling he cared as much about his father as he did about the death of his best friend."

Barrett let out a slow breath.

"He"—I swallowed and refused to look at Sasha—"wanted to destroy me because my father killed his brother. And because you and I—we once…"

"Mess," Barrett murmured. "God damn mess."

"It's a mess we'll worry about later," Sasha snapped. "Right now, we've got bigger problems to worry about."

"Bigger problems?" I demanded, finally facing him, facing the man whom I loved who didn't love me back. Who'd walked away from *us*. "What could possibly be a bigger problem?"

Sasha gestured with his chin. "Street is closed. And the local police are stopping cars."

"No," I whispered.

"*Da*," Sasha said, tone dark. "Your husband knows I'm here."

Chapter 6

SASHA

I'd killed a lot of men. Tortured my fair share too. Not because I'd wanted to, or got off on it in any way, but when you held a position of power, people had to know you couldn't be fucked with.

I was suddenly swarmed with ideas—creative, inventive ideas of how I was going to rip Ori Marino apart. That, I relished.

He'd seduced Quinn, married her, all orchestrated masterfully in his grand plot for revenge.

I knew a thing or two about revenge. I was fucking Russian.

"What do we do?" Quinn asked. Her voice was shaky. "I can't go back there. I won't."

Before I knew what I was doing, I reached over and set my hand on her thigh and gave it a squeeze. "You think I'm going to let that happen?"

I felt her body instantly relax under my touch.

"You have your piece?" I asked Barrett.

"Yup."

"Good. Now point it at Quinn—and follow my lead.

You"—I looked at Quinn and flashed her an arrogant grin —"pretend we kidnapped you."

She let out a breath but then nodded. "Okay."

The Italian policeman waved us up. I rolled to a stop and lowered my window. "Problem, officer?" I asked in Italian with a wide smile.

The young man in uniform peered into the car. He looked at Quinn and recognition flashed on his face before his eyes slid to Barrett's pistol.

"No, no problem," he said with a wave of his hand to let us through.

I rolled up the window and floored it. Out of the rearview mirror, I caught the officer pulling out a cell phone, no doubt to call Ori Marino.

"You can put the gun away now," Quinn said.

"Sorry," Barrett said. "That was too easy."

"He wanted to make sure," I said.

"Make sure?" Quinn asked.

"That it was me who came for you."

"So he didn't really let me go, did he?" Quinn looked out the window, and I couldn't see the expression on her face. "He won't give up."

"Neither do I."

She let out a strangled laugh. "Yeah. You don't give up. That's priceless."

Unresolved tension settled in the car—along with silence. And then Barrett broke it when she said, "This is going to be a fun plane ride home. On that note, can you go faster?"

"I'm doing ninety," I muttered.

"Fuck, in that case, slow down and pull over. You shouldn't be driving."

"I can drive fine," I snapped.

"You're blind in one eye. I should be driving."

"I'll slow down, but I'm not giving up the driver's seat," I stated, easing off the gas.

At some point, Barrett fell asleep in the back seat. Quinn took to staring out the window. I wanted to watch her, drink her in, but I'd just been reminded that I had only one good eye, and I needed it to ensure we didn't crash. I got us to the tarmac in one piece—just as the sun was beginning to set.

Barrett tiredly trudged toward the plane, her limp pronounced. I'd hear hell from Campbell—but it wasn't like anyone could ever tell Barrett what to do.

Quinn got out of the car and stared up at the plane, almost like she wasn't seeing it. Then she smiled. "Been a while since I've seen this plane." She squared her shoulders and went to board.

I took a moment to admire the sight of her. Despite her dirt-stained white dress and black boots, which didn't match, she looked regal and beautiful.

But I knew if I tried to touch her, hold her, she'd rebel. I had a lot of ground to make up for, and she wouldn't give in easily. Still, rescuing her on her wedding day to a tyrant probably went a long way.

I climbed the stairs after her. Barrett was already seated and sipping on a glass of Scotch. "Brandon called. He should be here in about twenty. I told him if he wasn't, then he could find his own way back to Dornoch. We have precious cargo." She shot Quinn a smile.

Quinn gave her one back and then looked at me, the smile slipping. She tightened her seat belt and looked out the window.

I sat next to her because I refused to be ignored.

She sighed.

"Are you sure we can't leave Kilmartin?" I demanded. "I'm ready to get the hell out of Italy."

Barrett snorted but didn't deign to reply. We were both exhausted, and I knew the moment she finished her Scotch and numbed out, she'd fall asleep.

"Will you look at me, Quinn?" When she refused, I added, "Please?"

Reluctantly, she faced me, but her eyes didn't meet mine. She stared at a spot over my shoulder. She was pale —she'd always been fair, but her skin looked wan. And there were smudges of tiredness beneath her eyes.

"When was the last time you really slept?"

Her eyes slipped back to mine. "It's been a few days."

"I just need to know one thing—and the rest I'll wait on."

She swallowed. "What?"

"Did he hurt you?" I pitched my voice low, soft.

Her green eyes shone bright with unshed tears. "Yes, Sasha. He hurt me."

"He put his hands on you?"

Quinn smiled, but it was sad. "And you still don't get it, do you?"

"Get what?"

"I wish he'd put his hands on me. It would've been easier." She shook her head and then wiped the tears that escaped the corners of her eyes. "There are so many worse things than a slap to the face or a kick to a rib. He made me hope. Ori Marino made me hope."

Chapter 7
QUINN

I could tell the moment he understood. Ori had given me hope and happiness. When I didn't know who I was, he'd promised we'd have a beautiful life together. A picture-perfect life.

Blissfully ignorant. That's what I'd been.

Part of me felt like a fool, that he'd played me so well. But I realized I'd never stood a chance against a master manipulator. He'd dangled a perfect carrot. Family, children, a loving husband. Days of sunshine and laughter, nights of passion and whispered endearments.

Oh, yes, Ori Marino knew which lies to spin like gold.

I'd fallen for every one of them.

When my memory came back, I was more broken than before. I'd been contending with the grief of my father's passing. I'd been coming to grips with Sasha leaving me.

What I hadn't been prepared for? The bursting of the magical bubble.

Ori was handsome and charming. A snake in a suit. And though he wanted revenge, he didn't ever use brute force with me. Instead, he'd shown me kindness, vulnerability. Intimacy.

That was the biggest betrayal of all.

Even if it had been all a game to him, it hadn't been for me. I'd fallen for it, fallen for his charm—and him.

Now that I knew myself, I was divided. Mentally, I knew Ori was a monster. Emotionally…emotionally I was nothing but scrambled feelings.

I loved two men.

Both were weak and strong.

Both used me, needed me, discarded me.

Now was not the time to discuss any of that, but I needed to say something.

"I won't absolve you," I whispered so Barrett didn't hear me.

"I know," he said, his own voice tempered.

Thankfully, our moment was interrupted by Brandon's arrival. His hair was a mess, and his clothes were disheveled.

"Holy fuck, I've never felt so alive!" he yelled in excitement. He saw me and marched over to my seat. "Get up and hug me!"

I unlatched my seat belt and then launched myself into his arms. I'd known Brandon since I was a teenager, and I'd once had a crush on him.

Sasha growled.

I clung to Brandon tighter and longer, just to piss off Sasha. Brandon knew my game. He laughed and patted my back.

"Damn, I wasn't sure we were going to be able to pull that off." Brandon released me and then looked at Barrett. "Where's the flight attendant? I need a drink."

"Sit down so we can take off," Sasha demanded.

Brandon grabbed my hand and dragged me to the

back of the plane. I smiled at him in relief. We sat down and buckled ourselves in.

A moment later, the door to the airplane shut. While the pilot was clearing our takeoff, a woman in a smart plaid skirt and matching jacket came down the aisle to ask us what we wanted to drink. I heard Sasha order a vodka. Brandon asked for Irish whiskey, and I requested a seltzer.

We sipped in silence, the lights of the plane dimmed, and then we were rolling down the tarmac. I didn't breathe a sigh of relief until we were in the air, flying away from Italy. I wanted as much distance between Ori and me as possible. And even though I'd told Sasha I didn't want to go to Scotland, I was actually relieved that I wouldn't be going back to Boston for the time being.

I did need to make a few calls. My friends had to know what was going on. So did Donovan. My brother hadn't been in Boston for months, and I was suddenly grateful for his inability to stay put. I'd ask Donovan to handle that conversation. Not to mention, I needed to call Harrison at O'Malley Properties and explain my disappearance and ask him to keep the fires burning.

Brandon reached over to grab my hand. "How are you doing?"

I let out a strangled laugh. "I don't even know. How are you here? Why are you here?"

He stretched out his long legs, and I noticed his pants were covered in soot. "I was with Barrett when Petrovich called. I had to come on your rescue mission." He winked and then his teasing fled. "You had us pretty fucking worried."

"Yeah. I can imagine," I murmured. I looked out the plane window. Stars littered the sky. How was it night already? It seemed like I'd been awake for days. This morning I'd gotten married. Now, I was fleeing my husband.

"Troubled?" Brandon asked knowingly.

"Putting it mildly."

He offered me his drink, but I shook my head. I closed my eyes. There was so much to sort through. My feelings for Ori. My feelings for Sasha.

"If I know one thing about Petrovich, it's that he'd die to protect you," Brandon said. "That doesn't make him all bad."

I only knew too well the things Sasha had suffered in order to protect me.

"He's ugly as fuck," he said mildly. "Not nearly pretty enough to hang on your arm."

"He's not," I said, my voice soft. "He's…"

"I know love is blind, but seriously."

"I was just going to say that he's Sasha. Burned or not."

Brandon took my hand and kissed my knuckles. "He doesn't deserve you."

I cracked a winsome smile. "I want him anyway."

Chapter 8
QUINN

Two hours later, we got off the plane in Dornoch. I'd been to Barrett and Flynn's home a handful of times. They'd remodeled an old castle, and that alone was worth contending with the weather.

The four of us piled into a waiting black town car. Barrett took the seat next to me and awkwardly slumped down and stretched out her right leg. She grimaced in discomfort but didn't complain. Still, it was easy to see the lines of pain bracketing her mouth.

"You should've had more Scotch," Sasha said, directing the comment to Barrett.

"I'd prefer it if my children didn't see me drunk out of my gourd," she fired back.

Clearly, she wasn't in too much agony that she couldn't give Sasha shit—which I enjoyed immensely.

Barrett reached over and grasped my hand. "The kids will be glad to see you."

"Do they even remember me?" I blurted out. It had been at least a year since I'd seen the three Campbell boys.

Barrett fell silent.

My eyes met Sasha's. He was staring at me with a look I couldn't decipher. I hated that I showed my emotions so easily, but Sasha never did. He was good at hiding.

I looked away from him to stare out the window. Thankfully, no one else tried to fill the silence. The gray sky and the angry rainstorm made it almost impossible to see anything. It was all a wet blur.

It was clear we were all exhausted. I knew I hadn't slept much the last few days, and judging by the tiredness and bags under the eyes of the others, neither had they.

"Thank you," I said quietly, making sure to look at each of them. Even Sasha, whose gaze I held the longest. "For coming for me."

"Glad to do it, lass," Brandon said with a roguish grin. "I was getting bored. I needed a good adventure."

"You're an ass," Barrett quipped, but a small smile played about her lips. She pulled out her cell phone from her black jacket pocket and shot off a text. "So Flynn knows to expect us."

"Can I borrow your phone?" I asked. "I need to call some people."

"I'd prefer if you waited," Sasha voiced.

"Would you?" I purred.

Brandon looked out the window and Barrett kept her head down. Neither one of them wanted to get in the middle of the brewing storm. Because I had no desire—or energy—for a shouting match, I retracted. As soon as I was in private and had a moment, I'd demand a phone.

Ten minutes later, the car turned down the road that led up to Dornoch Castle. It was on one thousand acres of land, and the Campbells' closest neighbor was Barrett's best friend, Ash.

The car stopped and the doors opened. Servants came down from the house carting umbrellas. We were escorted into the castle, which smelled of wood smoke and comfort.

Two hounds—and an ewe—ran forward to greet us. I expected Barrett's sons to follow suit, but when they didn't show, I asked, "Where are your kids?"

"No idea," Barrett admitted. "Do you know where they are, Christopher?" She looked to the butler for an answer.

"With Barnabas. And then Mr. Campbell asked if Mr. and Mrs. Buchanan could keep them for the evening."

"Is anyone hungry?" Barrett asked, handing off her coat to Christopher.

"I could eat," Brandon admitted.

While they discussed food, I sank to the floor and stroked the sheep. Betty had been a gift from Barnabas, an old Scottish farmer, a few years ago. Flynn hadn't wanted her, but he couldn't deny Barrett anything.

"Quinn?" Sasha asked.

I looked up at him. "I just got really tired."

Barrett nodded. "I'm going to show you to your guest room, and then I'll have food sent up to everyone. We all need a few hours of sleep."

Sasha held out his hand. I looked at it and then reluctantly took it. He lifted me slowly, his ice blue eyes delving into mine.

When I was standing on my own, he dropped my hand but still stood close. It took all of my willpower not to lean into him.

"Show me the way," I said to Barrett.

She started for the stairs, her movements slow, her hip tight. She let out a hiss of pain. "Christopher, will you please have Mary bring me a bottle of SINNERS and a glass?"

"Yes, of course."

"It's going to be a long night," she muttered.

"Where's Flynn?" I asked as I trailed behind Barrett.

"Meeting," she said. She didn't expound, and I didn't expect her to, which meant it was probably something political.

We got to the second floor, and Barrett pointed to the two rooms across from each other. "You and you," she said, directing her statement to Sasha and Brandon. She looked at me and grinned. "I saved you the best room… It has the best bathroom. It rivals the master bath."

"Why does she get it?" Brandon whined, sounding like a petulant teenager.

"Don't start with me. I don't have any patience left," Barrett stated. "I'll see you both in a few hours."

Brandon went into one of the rooms and shut the door. Sasha took a moment longer. Hand on the knob, he looked at me, "If you need anything…"

"She won't," Barrett said with a raise of her eyebrows. She grasped my arm and urged me away. I heard the door to Sasha's room click shut.

"I don't need you fighting my battles," I said to her.

She snorted. "You wear your emotions on your face. If I hadn't been standing right there, you would've gone into his arms and crawled into his bed—and I know you don't want more confusion to muddle through."

I thought about disagreeing with her, but what was the point? I did want Sasha. I was angry and frustrated, and my heart hurt. But at the end of the day, he was my home. When he left me, he destroyed my home, and I hadn't been the same since.

I wasn't sure that was ever going to go away. Even if we reconciled. Even if we ruined each other. All I knew was I couldn't live like this—in limbo.

Chapter 9
QUINN

"Here we go," Barrett said when we got to the end of the hallway. She opened the bedroom door and gestured for me to go inside.

"It's so...pink," I said, mouth agape. "Is that—French lace?"

"It is," she said with a grin. She closed the door and then waved me toward the bathroom. "You've got to see this."

The bathroom was even more decadent. A glass shower with four sprays and a separate Jacuzzi tub.

"Is this all new?" I wondered. "I don't remember this."

"We remodeled it last year."

"It's girly. You're not girly."

"No," she agreed with a smile. "But I know a lot of women who are, and I thought it would be nice for them to stay in this room when they came."

Tears pricked at my eyes. "You remodeled this bedroom for me?"

"I don't know what you're talking about." She stared at me for a long moment and then, "Oh, honey, come here."

I went into her arms and cried against her shoulder. Exhaustion eventually won out over terror, but there was still a healthy dose of that too.

"What am I going to do?" I whispered, trying to get my breathing under control.

Barrett pulled back. "First, you're going to take a bath. I'm going to find you some clothes to change into, and then you're going to sleep. You're going to sleep with no alarms. When you wake up, we'll have a plan."

"We?" I sniffed.

"We. Sasha, Brandon, Flynn, and I. Hell, we might involve Duncan because he's good at planning too."

I let out a laugh. "And what about me? Am I just supposed to sit on the sidelines and watch my life happen without me?"

Barrett didn't reply. Instead, she turned, slowly, and went into the bathroom.

"Get in here," she commanded as she reached for the tub faucet.

Her tone didn't bother me. Barrett telling me what to do didn't feel the same as Ori and Sasha telling me what to do.

The bathroom was filling with steam and the scent of honeysuckle. I glanced at myself in the mirror and blanched. My eyes looked tired, and my skin was wan, I had scratches and dirt along my arms. My throat was blotchy with forming bruises. I leaned closer to examine them.

"What happened?" Barrett asked.

I met her hazel eyes in the glass. "Ori's cousin. Tried to strangle me."

She swiped her tongue across her full lips. "A woman?"

I nodded.

"Probably the only reason you're still alive."

"You used to be a gentle person," I reminded her with a startled laugh.

"I used to be a lot of things. I think we've been too soft with you, Quinn," she said.

I looked down at my left hand. The engagement ring and wedding band glinted in the bathroom light.

"May I see?" she asked quietly.

"Why?"

"Curiosity."

I gave her my hand, and she lifted it and peered at the ring set.

"Well, the bastard has good taste," she said. "I'll give him that."

"What do I do, Barrett?" I asked. "I'm married, but in name only."

"Only you can make that call." She gently cropped my hand. "It's okay, you know."

"What's okay?"

"To miss him. To miss Ori."

I blanched. "I don't miss—"

"I missed Igor. When I first got back."

"You did?"

She nodded and then walked over to turn off the tub faucet. "I was deeply conflicted. For a long time after. He changed me. There's nothing wrong with admitting that."

"I care—cared—for him. And it feels disloyal and sick to even say."

"Do you mind if I sit? My hip is killing me."

"Go ahead. Do you mind if I get in the bath?" I reached for one of my boots.

"Nope." She looked down at her own hands, her thumb tracing the delicate band on her slightly bent ring finger.

She didn't wear an engagement ring. Barrett held it up

to show me. "The ring belonged to Flynn's mother. I was terrified that after Igor broke my finger I wouldn't be able to wear the ring again." She shrugged and shook her head.

"It's beautiful," I said, kicking off my other boot. I unzipped the zipper on the side of the dress and shrugged out of it. I wasn't modest, so I removed my bra and underwear, but Barrett discreetly looked away, giving me space.

"I understand you, Quinn," she said. "I understand what happened to you. I understand how you could have feelings for Ori. It makes perfect sense to me actually."

"Then do you care to explain it?" I reached for the brand-new loofa and bar of soap resting on the edge of the tub. "Because I sure as hell don't get it."

"He left you," she said, her voice soft. "Sasha left all of us. But I had Flynn and the bairns. You had no one."

I swallowed, hating how blunt she was, but knowing it was the truth. Embarrassment burned bright in my cheeks. Sasha had left me. I'd been alone and everyone had known it.

"You were vulnerable. You had no armor."

"I didn't realize I needed any," I admitted, scraping the loofa against my skin. "Ori…he wasn't just nice to me. Anyone can be nice. It was how he looked at me. Like he wanted to know every part of me. Like he wanted to give me all the happiness I'd been missing. He wanted to give me children."

I heard Barrett's inhalation, but I didn't look at her as I kept talking.

"It's hard to reconcile the man he showed me with the man he actually is."

"He's both. Igor was both. Ruthless. Determined to bring down Flynn. But aside from breaking my finger, he never physically hurt me."

"Those are the worst kind of scars, aren't they?" I asked. "The ones that don't leave a mark on your skin."

She sighed. "Yeah, Quinn. Those are the worst kind of scars."

"Do they fade? With time?" I finally looked at her. Her hazel eyes were bright with emotion.

"No. They don't fade. You just learn to live with the scar tissue."

Chapter 10
QUINN

Barrett left and I sat in the water until it went cold. Finally, I stood up and reached for the white towel hanging on the rack. My muscles were lax and loose, and I hoped the tray of food had arrived, so I could eat and then crawl into bed.

I wrapped the towel around me and then opened the drain. As the sound of the water rushed out of the tub, I opened the door and squeaked in surprise.

Sasha was sitting on the bed, ice blue gaze trained on me.

Suddenly nervous, I looked around for a robe—anything to cover my body. Because at the moment, he looked at me like I was naked. Lust and love battled in his eyes.

Goosebumps elicited along my skin. I remembered how it felt to be touched by him. The graze of his teeth, the skating of his hands.

He looked freshly showered, the close-cropped blond hair on the left side of his head was probably dry by now.

"What are you doing here?" I asked, hating that my voice was breathless.

"I wanted to talk. Without the others." He stood up and stalked toward me. I backed up a step. Sasha stopped. "Easy. I just wanted to see the bruises on your neck." He paused. "Okay?"

I nodded because I couldn't answer.

His hands were gentle when they cupped my face. He angled my chin up, and then his thumbs brushed along my neck. I couldn't stop the shiver that worked its way down my body. His eyes met mine. He noticed my reaction to his touch, yet he didn't say anything.

"What happened?" he asked.

I swallowed, wanting him to back off and pull me closer at the same time. "Ori's cousin. She tried to—ah—stop me. From leaving."

"How'd you get away?"

"Rock to her head." I briefly wondered if she was all right, but I didn't really care about her. Not after what she'd done to me.

He dropped his hands but didn't make a move to stand back.

"My turn," I whispered. I reached out and touched his right cheek. It was rough with abrasions. When he'd been recovering from the fire burns, he'd had a few skin grafts to the face, but he hadn't stuck around, so I hadn't been able to see how it had healed.

"What do you think?" he asked, tone gruff. "Am I hideous?"

"No," I said quietly. My eyes lifted to meet his. "You were never hideous. Not to me."

"My body looks worse. The grafts didn't take as well there." He took a step back and unbuttoned his shirt. He removed it and tossed it aside.

"It bothers you," I stated. I couldn't stop myself from

touching him, my hand dragging across his chest to rest on his heart.

He placed his hand on mine. "It did. For a very long time."

"What changed?"

"Distance."

I tried to take my hand back, but he wouldn't let me. "You needed distance. From me," I said, unable to keep the acid from my tone.

"Stop," he said when I began to struggle, trying to free myself. "I haven't felt your touch in—Please, don't stop touching me."

The aching, raw vulnerability in his voice nearly did me in, but somehow, I found the steel in my spine.

"No. You don't get to do this. Not now. Not here."

"Quinn," he begged.

"You left me!" I cried out, choking on a sob. "You left me, and my dad died, and I lost…" My head dipped, so I wouldn't be forced to look him in the eyes. They were somber, and it would be my undoing. He always had a way of looking at me, stripping away everything that I was.

"Lost our baby?" he asked.

I slowly lifted my head. Sasha reached out and swiped away the tears cascading down my cheeks with his thumb.

"How did you know?" I asked.

"I went to Boston," he said. "I talked to Shannon."

"Oh." I bit my lip.

"I was mad," he admitted with a sardonic laugh. "Enraged. How could you not tell me, Quinn?"

"How was I supposed to find you?" I demanded. "You'd left already. Disappeared."

"You could've told Barrett…or Dimitri."

Somehow, he'd pulled me to him, and I was flush against his chest. I pressed my cheek to his warm skin because I was only human. And maybe I wanted his comfort—maybe I wanted to offer him my own.

"I didn't want you to come back because of obligation. And I know you, that's exactly what you would've done."

He wrapped his arms around me, and I breathed him in and closed my eyes.

"I'm so fucking sorry, Quinn. I'm so sorry you had to go through that alone."

"I wasn't alone," I said automatically.

"Right. You had your father and Shannon. But you should've had me."

"We should've had a lot of things," I stated sadly.

"We could have them."

"Don't promise me anything, Sasha." I pulled back so I could look him in the face. "Not right now. Not when all this stuff with Ori is looming over us. Don't make promises you're not ready to keep."

"Do you still love me?"

"Do you still love me?" I echoed.

"I never stopped," he admitted.

"How the hell am I supposed to trust you ever again?"

"Trust is a lot like faith, don't you think? You either have it or you don't."

When I moved to take a step back, he finally let me. "I don't have either. Not where we're concerned."

His smile surprised me, and then he leaned over and placed a gentle kiss on the end of my nose. "You don't have to worry. I have enough for both of us."

Chapter 11
QUINN

There was a knock on the door, and a moment later, it opened. Barrett stepped inside and stopped. "Oops. Sorry. Didn't know I was interrupting something."

"You're interrupting nothing," Sasha said with a heated look that seared me to my core.

He turned and left.

Barrett watched him go and then focused her attention on me. "What the hell did I just walk in on?"

"I have no idea," I said with a sigh.

She shook her head. "I brought you some of my clothes. The sweats will be a little short on you, but they'll do." She set them on the bed. "You okay?"

"I think so."

"I didn't hear any yelling," Barrett pressed.

"No yelling."

"Hmm."

"What does that mean?" I demanded, finally going over to the clothes. I needed to lose the towel.

"I expected gunfire."

I changed quickly and didn't reply. Frankly, I was all

talked out. I climbed beneath the covers of the white coverlet and sighed. "This is amazing."

My eyes drifted shut, and I faintly heard the sound of the door closing. I fell asleep and didn't dream. When I awoke a few hours later, it was completely dark outside, and for a moment, I'd forgotten where I was.

Rolling over, I stretched my body as I slowly came to. My stomach rumbled, reminding me that I hadn't eaten since I'd choked down toast that morning.

The morning of my wedding.

With sleep came clarity and the ability to think about the consequences. Ori would try to come for me, of that I had no doubt. I was his wife, and he viewed me as chattel.

I shivered when I thought about ever coming face to face with him again. No doubt he wanted to make me pay for leaving him. Or make those I loved pay.

After using the restroom, I padded downstairs in search of food and people. Everyone was already awake and in the library.

Barrett and Flynn sat next to each other on one of the couches. Sasha and Brandon were on the other. Their heads turned when I entered.

Flynn got up from his spot and came to me. Before I could get a word out, he engulfed me in a hug. "Glad to have you back safe and sound, lass," he whispered gruffly.

I pressed my cheek to his gray sweater and closed my eyes. He smelled of pipe tobacco and Scotch When he pulled back, he looked at me. "Are you hungry?"

"Yes."

He led me to the chair near the fire and urged me to sit down. "Something to drink?"

"Water, please."

"You sure you don't want something stronger?" he asked. "You might need it."

"Water," I insisted.

I stared into the flames of the fire while Flynn got me a glass. Barrett made a move to get up, but he urged her to sit. "You don't move. Rest the hip. I'll tell the cook to get Quinn a plate."

Flynn left the library, and it was suddenly too quiet. "How long have you guys been awake?" I asked.

They all exchanged a look.

"None of you slept," I said with a sigh.

"Too wired," Brandon said by way of explanation.

Sasha's gaze found mine. The firelight cast half of him in shadow. One bright blue eye tracked me.

"What have you guys been talking about?" I asked.

"Let's wait for Flynn," Barrett said. "There's a lot we need to discuss."

"Rethinking the drinking?" Brandon asked.

"Maybe." I took a sip of water and forced myself to look away from Sasha. We were two magnets inevitably drawn to one another. I loved him, but I also didn't trust him.

Flynn returned and said, "Food will be ready in a few. In the meantime, we should probably talk. Anyone's drink need refreshing?"

The three of them raised their near-empty glasses.

"Well, what do I look like, your host?" Flynn asked with a laugh. "You know where the liquor cart is. Don't worry, hen, I'll get your drink for you."

Once everyone's glasses were full and the cook brought me a plate of food, we got down to business.

"Well, Quinn, it seems you've gotten yourself into a little bit of trouble," Flynn stated. His tone was mild, curious.

"If you mean, did I go and get married to an Italian

monster who wants Sasha dead, then yeah, I'd call that trouble," I remarked just as dryly.

"He thinks I killed Igor," Sasha added. "And I think for all parties concerned, it needs to stay that way. Marino does not need to know Barrett's involvement."

"Agreed," Flynn said. "Does he know that I was there the night his father died? Because we already know he wants you dead. I've got to know if he wants me dead."

"He never mentioned you," I said.

"I don't know whether to be relieved or offended," Flynn remarked.

Barrett handed him her Scotch. "You would think that."

"He knows I left with Sasha," I said.

"He let you leave," Sasha voiced. "He knew we were coming, and he let you escape."

"I need to call Shannon," I stated. "Immediately. I have to let her know—"

"Already taken care of." Sasha took a sip of vodka. "I had men in place before we even came to Italy. Shannon and Patrick are protected as are Richard and Adam, along with their baby daughter."

"And my brother?" I asked.

"Still in London. He's fine. Though to be honest, I'm not even sure he's on Marino's radar."

I blinked and then relief curled through me. "Thank you."

He raised his eyebrows.

"What? Did you expect me to yell at you for being so highhanded?"

"A little, yeah," he teased.

I grinned. "Well, I hate to disappoint you."

"Who said I was disappointed?"

Brandon groaned. "Really? Is this what it's going to be like from now on? I need a rubbish bin if this continues."

"Can I ask a question?" I set my fork down on the plate and turned my body away from the flames. "Does anyone have an idea of how to get me out of this marriage I'm trapped in?"

"You were coerced into marriage when you weren't in a sound frame of mind. It won't hold up in court," Barrett said.

"You know how slow all that bureaucratic bullshit takes to get turned over," Sasha said. "I have another idea."

I leaned forward. "I'm listening."

He grinned, but it wasn't friendly. "I'm going to make you a widow."

Chapter 12
SASHA

Her eyes widened and she swallowed. But there was no point in beating around the bush. The bastard wanted to send a message. Well, then I'd send another right back. And then I'd be taking his life as payment.

Barrett and Flynn were whispering to each other, but I paid them no attention, my focus solely on Quinn. She was beautiful in firelight. Her short dark hair accentuated her cheekbones and made her eyes flicker like green flames.

I missed the long hair, though. You couldn't wrap your fingers through short hair.

God, I just wanted to be inside her and ease the ache between us.

It nearly tore her apart when we talked about the baby —about our son. We had only just touched on it. I needed more from her. I wanted to hear everything she went through, every emotion, every body change. I'd never get that time back with her.

Did we have a future?

A ringing cell phone jarred me from my thoughts. It was mine. I got up and took the call out of the library.

It was Dimitri.

"How's Quinn?" he asked.

"She's…" I tried to run my hand through my hair only to remember that I had very little of it. "Holding on."

"That's good. That's good," he repeated. "What's the plan?"

"I need you in the old Italian territory. See who can be bought. See who can be swayed. I need information on Ori Marino. If you have to, go to his mother's restaurant."

"And do what exactly? Hurt an old woman?"

"No, you *piz`da*. Actually, I have a better idea. Find out who holds the lease. Buy it from them."

"What if the Marinos own the building?"

"Then buy the mortgage."

He sighed. "If I can't…"

"Then we'll come up with another plan. You got her friends out of Boston?"

"*Da*. The four of them—and the baby—are on your island."

In case shit ever hit the fan, and I'd needed a place to go and hunker down off the map, I'd wanted sanctuary. Only Dimitri knew about the place. I hadn't even told Quinn about it. I'd wanted to take her there. One day…

"Shannon wasn't too happy about being uprooted from her life. Not when she discovered Quinn was in danger. Her husband made her see reason, though."

"And Adam and Richard?"

"Charming gentlemen. Complimented me on my suit."

I let out a chuckle and then sobered. "Hopefully it won't have to be for long. What about Donovan?"

"He wouldn't go. Craggy bastard. He said he wasn't leaving Quinn on her own. We almost got into it."

"Almost?"

"He would've killed me," Dimitri joked. "The old

grump loves Quinn like a daughter. I backed off. I've got three men watching him."

"He won't like that."

"Well, Quinn won't like it if Donovan winds up dead. I'll take my chances with him."

"And Sean?"

"Told him to lay low. Since he's out of the country, and he and Quinn aren't close, I doubt Marino will go after him. You coming back to New York? Boston?"

"Not sure yet."

"All right." He sighed. "You sure you don't want my help?"

"I have your help. In the way I need it," I said.

"I wish I was there to watch your back."

"I can watch my own back."

Dimitri snorted. "Bullshit. I'll be in touch when I have news about the building."

We hung up, and I stuck my phone inside my pocket. I turned to find Quinn in the hallway, staring at me with questioning green eyes.

"Dimitri?" she inquired.

I nodded. "Your friends and family are safe."

She let out a sigh of relief. "Good. Thank you."

We gazed at each other for a long moment. I could hear the faintest sounds of voices in the library, but I ignored them, choosing to focus on the woman in front of me.

Did she feel it too? This loss and anger, but the hope that never burned out?

"Stop looking at me that way," she said quietly.

"What way is that?"

"Like I'm broken and pathetic."

I raised an eyebrow. "You're projecting."

"Maybe," she allowed. She looked behind her. Exhaustion tugged at her limbs. Even though she'd slept, it hadn't been enough. She needed me to hold her so she could fall into a deep sleep and not be worried that Marino was coming for her.

"Come on," I said, holding out my hand.

She peered at it like it was some unknown entity. I was trying to be patient so I wouldn't overwhelm her. Eventually she put her hand in mine, and I walked her through the kitchen toward the back of the house.

The castle was on the edge of Dornoch Firth and a rocky outcrop. The entire back wall of the kitchen was one long window. Barrett's favorite place in the entire house was seated at the kitchen table while she watched storms and waves unleash their rage against the stones. Stones that stood the test of time, took the anger, took it all.

That's how I felt. I was one of those boulders, and no matter what Quinn threw at me, I'd absorb it. I'd even ask for more.

"Tea?" I asked her.

She nodded, her eyes on the ocean. It was gray and dark except for the brief flashes of lightning that illuminated the sky. I found it comforting and even enjoyed the grumbling of the thunderstorm.

"Tell me what happened," I said as I plugged in the electric teakettle.

"When?"

"From the moment I left. Tell me about your life."

"Will you tell me about yours?"

"Of course." I looked at her. "Please, Quinn? I need to know it all."

Chapter 13
QUINN

"Where do you want me to start?" I asked, my voice harsh. "From the moment I woke up to find you gone? Or the lovely note you left me?"

His mouth tightened, and then he said, "All of it. I can take it."

"Take it," I repeated. "God all fucking mighty. You rat bastard."

Suddenly, he grinned—which only enraged me more. "Why are you smiling? I'm ready to do you some serious bodily harm for the way you treated me."

He threw his head back and laughed. It was an easy sound, so full of joy. I couldn't remember the last laugh we'd shared. It was hard to laugh when the man you loved was lying burned and broken in a bed. It was hard to laugh when you saw the desire to live leave his eyes. It was hard to laugh when he left you.

"There's your spark," he said. His smile dimmed but didn't disappear. His eyes were bright blue, the color of ice.

They looked anything but cold.

"I was worried we wouldn't be able to find it, but it's

all coming back. I think in a few days, you might even feel like yourself. And I can't wait for that, Quinn. So please. Yell, cry, scream. Hit me, kick me, do whatever you have to do, but in the end please forgive me." His voice was earnest, solemn. "I hate myself for hurting you —if I thought there could have been any other way, I would've stayed. I would've stayed and worked through it all, but I needed to find a new self. When I was burned" —he swallowed—"it wasn't just my body that was ruined. Do you understand? Please tell me you understand."

"That morning you left… I woke up thinking we'd turned a corner, that we'd finally made it. That we'd gotten through the shit and the pain. We'd gone through the hardest part." I shook my head. "Do you know what it was like waking up in our bed—your side was cold. I remember that. I remember thinking you got up and you'd made coffee. I thought we'd sit together, share breakfast, laugh quietly. Make love on the kitchen counter."

I thought about the other man I'd done that with. I swallowed and blocked it out.

"And then that note. That God damn note telling me that what we had was dead and that you were gone and not coming back. I smashed all the plates, all the glassware we'd picked out together. And then I walked out of that apartment and out of that life. I cried myself to sleep so many nights," I whispered. "So many tears I wondered how I still had any left. I cried for you. I cried for me."

I glanced at him. His eyes were on mine, sad, bright, looking like he wanted to shed tears of his own.

"We were both hurting," I said, trying to be strong, trying not to be the woman who always broke down. "When you were in that bed, we both were hurting, Sasha. I hurt worse when you left me."

The teakettle whistled, and Sasha unplugged it to pour out the water. "Mint? Chamomile?"

"Chamomile."

He placed the bag in the boiling water and then brought me the mug. He set it down in front of me and then pulled out the kitchen chair that was next to mine and took a seat. Thankfully, he made no move to touch me. I didn't think I could handle him touching me, not when I was this raw, this open.

I grasped the mug in my hands, enjoying the warmth on my cold fingers.

"What happened when you got home to Boston?" he wondered.

"Dad took me in." I'd stayed in bed for days. I wouldn't shower or eat. Not until Shannon came over and pulled me out of it. "A few weeks later, I found out I was pregnant."

"Were you upset about it?"

I shook my head, dark hair falling across my cheek. I brushed it back. "It was the only thing worth living for. *He*," I corrected.

Sasha reached out and gently removed one of my hands from my tea mug. He laced his fingers through mine, his thumb stroking my knuckle. "Shannon took me to see his headstone."

I swallowed a lump of tears.

"Ciaran. I'm saying it wrong, aren't I? How do you pronounce it? His name?"

"Keer-in."

Sasha repeated the name, familiarizing his Russian tongue with the Irish name. "No one knew, did they?"

"Dad and Jessica. Shannon, Patrick, Adam, and Richard. No one else knew."

"Would you have told Barrett?"

"No. I'd cut her out. Cut her off. It was just too hard. She was never going to know."

"What would you have told him about me?"

"I don't know, Sasha," I said tiredly. "I thought I'd have about five years before I had to tell him anything about you."

"Do you have any pictures? Of you pregnant?"

"I did. Ori took my phone." My lips pursed. "Now you."

"Now me, what?"

"Your turn to share."

"Let's go back to the library. Sit by the fire. I'll tell you there."

Sasha stood, refusing to let go of my hand. With my other, I grabbed the mug of tea. We walked back to the library. It was empty save for the fire. Everyone else must've gone to bed. They must've realized that Sasha and I would want to talk—alone.

Sasha guided me to the couch closest to the fire. He urged me to sit down, and then he removed the plaid blanket from the back of the couch and covered me with it. He tucked it around me. "You warm?"

I nodded.

He took the couch across from me, almost like he needed the distance because he didn't trust himself not to touch me.

I wasn't sure if I wanted his touch or not.

"I went to Russia first. To the town I grew up in."

"I figured," I said with a nod.

"I went to the lake," he admitted.

"The lake where your brother drowned?"

"*Da.*" He ran a hand across his face. "I saw the fucking shack where I was born. I saw my father's grave and spit on it." Sasha leaned over and rested his arms on his thighs and looked down at the ground. "I needed to go back to the beginning, you know? Back to where all the pain started."

Sasha and I both had suffered in our childhood. I'd lost my mother as a teen and that had been terrible. But both my parents had loved me, protected me, sheltered me.

"Anyway. I spent a few weeks drunk on the cheapest, shittiest vodka. One day, I don't know, I'd had enough. I left Russia and went to Japan."

"Japan? That's a switch." I took a sip of the now tepid tea. The firelight gilded him in shadows. He looked like a beast, a brutalized animal. But he was still my Sasha.

He nodded. "I spent months training in the ancient art of the Samurai. I needed to retrain my body and my mind. I needed a new path."

I fell silent and digested his words. Finally, I asked, "Why did you come back?"

Sasha looked at me, his face softening. "You. I came back for you."

Chapter 14
QUINN

"Thank you for telling me," I said quietly.

"I want you so much, Quinn."

"Don't," I pleaded. "Don't do this. Not now. Not when—"

"There was no one else," he interrupted. "While I was away. While we were apart."

I let out a dry chuckle. "That doesn't matter."

"It doesn't?"

"We weren't together," I pointed out. "You were free to —if you wanted—"

"That's my point. I didn't want anyone else."

I'd been with Ori. He'd been inside of me. More importantly, he'd found a way into my heart. Now, it was all muddled.

"I don't care that you were with him," he said.

"Well, we both know that's a lie. How could you be okay with it? Your enemy?"

"Do I like it? No. But you did exactly what you were supposed to. I told you to move on. Am I supposed to punish you for that? For finding someone else? Does it grate more because it's him. *Da*—yes. But I don't hate you for it. Okay?"

I shook my head and set my mug of tea down on a slate gray coaster. "You've got a lot of nerve. You're not even *upset?* You're so forgiving. You're so understanding. Well, fuck you. I don't need your understanding." I flung the blanket off me and rose, feeling heat climb into my cheeks. "You forgive me for being with another man? What about loving another man? Do you forgive me for that?"

Sasha stood slowly, his eyes trained on me. "Do you want to do this? Accuse and fight? Because I can do that too."

"Let's go," I sneered. "Let's have it out because I can't keep having these moments with you. These beautiful perfect moments where I think I recognize the old you, only to realize that man's dead and this—this—*stranger* has taken his place!"

"You didn't tell me about the baby," he accused.

"Even if I'd wanted to tell you, how was I supposed to? You didn't leave a number. You'd told Barrett you went to Russia but not to Japan. And for the record, I couldn't stand the thought of her looking at me with anything resembling pity. I could handle being the woman you left. But not the pregnant woman you left. I have some pride."

He hung his head in shame. Sasha had claimed my spark had come back, but what about his? He was still feeling guilty over leaving me. And I wasn't sure I'd ever be able to stop blaming him for it. So here we were, trapped in an endless cycle of blame, guilt, and love.

I looked away from him to stare into the fire. "The day of Ciaran's funeral"—I swallowed hard—"my father stood by my side, holding the black umbrella over our heads. It was raining and everything just looked...gray. Gray sky. Gray headstone. Gray, gray, gray." I pulled my gaze away and finally let him see it—see me. The tears streamed down my cheeks. "He was there, and you weren't. And then he died, too. Why does every man I love leave me?"

Before I knew it, I was crushed against his firm chest. His hands were in my hair, and he was whispering endearments to me in Russian, his lips against my forehead. I cried uncontrollably. It was messy and jagged. Just when I thought I was getting fixed, something else broke me.

"Let me put the pieces back together, Quinn," he whispered.

I hadn't even been aware that I'd spoken the words aloud. Maybe I hadn't. Maybe Sasha had heard them anyway. Maybe we still understood each other after all this time apart.

"Will you let me?" he asked.

I shook my head and pulled away, away from his warmth and solidness, because I knew that it was all an illusion.

"Please, Quinn. I'll do anything for you. We'll handle Marino. We can start fresh and build a life—"

I placed my hand on his lips to stop him from speaking. And then I opened my mouth and shattered the last chance we had of ever being together again.

"I'm pregnant, Sasha."

Chapter 15
QUINN

His arms dropped from around me, and he took a step back. His blue eyes widened, and then he shook his head. "No," he whispered.

"Yes."

"No!" he roared in anguish.

It destroyed my heart. What was left of it.

"How?" he asked.

"When I had amnesia, we were together without—"

"It's too early to know," he stated. "Your amnesia didn't last for—"

"Not too early. I'm having symptoms."

He held up his hand. His eyes closed, like it physically pained him to look at me.

I fell silent and watched the love of my life collapse like a child onto the floor. He stared at the rug. I stared at him.

The grandfather clock chimed the hour of midnight. Midnight. The start of a new day. Only nothing about the day felt new or young. It was old and full of misery, full of impossible choices with improbable outcomes.

I would not give up the baby for a chance with Sasha.

I couldn't.

I'd already lost one child. I'd be damned if I lost another.

"I wish it could be different," I said to him, my tone soft, my heart breaking for him. For us.

He looked up slowly. Even when he'd been in the hospital near death, even when he'd survived and been stuck in a bed, I'd never seen him so defeated.

Sasha tried to speak, but nothing came out of his mouth. So he just nodded and went back to looking at the floor.

I finally sat down in the chair next to the fire. Perhaps he wanted to be alone to mourn the life we'd never have. But I didn't walk away, because I knew how it felt when the world came crashing down around you, when you trekked across uneven ground, wondering if the earth would open up and swallow you whole.

Eventually, I slept. I woke up briefly when I felt someone placing a blanket over me. Opening my eyes into slits, I saw Sasha. His face was ashen, his mouth pinched. His hand stroked my cheek, and he said something in Russian.

Myshka.

Little mouse.

I smiled softly and snuggled against his hand. I was fast asleep moments later.

When I awoke again, the weak early morning sunlight was streaming through the windows of the library, and the fire was nothing but ashes and hot coals.

I stretched my arms over my head. I blinked and yawned, feeling no more rested than I had the day before.

Emotion took its toll.

I looked to the couch. Sasha was sitting up, still in last

night's clothes. His bright blue eyes met mine. Exhaustion wore grooves at the corners of his mouth.

"Did you sleep?" I croaked.

He shook his head.

"You've been awake the entire night?"

"*Da.* I was watching you sleep. I…"

"What?" I pressed when he fell silent suddenly.

His mouth quirked up into a half smile, pulling the scarred skin taut. "I wanted to make sure you were really here."

"I'm here," I whispered.

"There were a lot of nights," he said in the still morning, "when I would be in bed. Exhausted, but unable to sleep. My body hurt. I could barely move. I'd take myself in my hand and think of you. Fall asleep with my seed on my stomach. I'd whisper words of love to you—wishing you were next to me to hear them."

"So you watched me sleep," I said in understanding.

"I watched you sleep," he agreed.

"Tell me now," I said urgently. "Tell me some of the things you told me those nights."

He spoke in Russian, the words flowing off his tongue. But I heard the yearning, the desire, the need to hold me.

I wanted to go to him, touch him, crawl into his arms and never leave. But I'd given up that right when I told him I was carrying another man's child.

"I love you, Quinn," he said in English. "And if you let me, I'll love the child like it was my own. He—or she—never has to know I'm not the father."

"Sasha," I whispered.

"I don't need an answer now. In fact, don't answer at all. I want you, *Myshka.* I've always wanted you. This doesn't change anything for me."

I shook my head. "This is—How can it not?"

"I walked away once," he reminded me. "We're here now because of me, love. Not because of you or anything you've done. I pushed you into his arms. I left you open, vulnerable. Let me love you. Let me protect you. Let me be the man you know I can be." His eyes drifted to my belly. "Let me be a father. Let's be a family."

His words were beautiful, and at one time I would've jumped into his arms without hesitation. But I was older now. Not wiser. God, not even a little bit wiser.

Sasha's smile was crooked. "Take your time, Quinn. I'm not going anywhere."

Chapter 16
SASHA

With one final look, Quinn threw off the blanket and stood up. She stretched her arms over her head.

I would never get tired of looking at her.

I'd wait. As long as it took. She needed to know I wasn't going anywhere. Time together would prove it.

She was about to say something when Barrett entered the library. She looked no better. It would take more than one good night of sleep to feel restored.

"Did you both sleep down here?" Barrett asked.

Quinn flushed. "I slept in the chair."

"I was on the couch," I said with a grin. "But I didn't sleep."

"You look like you've been awake all night," she agreed. "How about me? How old do I look?"

"Um," Quinn began.

"Forget it, I don't want to know." She groaned. "Breakfast?"

We both nodded and then followed Barrett into the kitchen. I caught Quinn yawning again. She hastily covered her mouth and grinned behind it when she saw I'd noticed.

Barrett put on the coffee and then went to the refrigerator and pulled out a quiche. She turned on the oven and while we waited for it to heat up, Quinn and I set the table.

"Where are the other men?" Quinn asked.

"Flynn is on a call, and Brandon is still sleeping," she explained. She opened the cupboard and grabbed a few mugs.

There was the sound of the back door slamming against the wall, and three young boys ran into the kitchen. Two of them were the spitting image of their father—cobalt blue eyes and dark hair. The quiet one—Noah—looked like Barrett with auburn hair and hazel eyes.

They dashed around the kitchen island, their laughter ringing out through the quiet morning. One by one, Barrett caught them each in her arms for a kiss before letting them go.

I looked at Quinn, who watched the children with an absent-minded tender smile on her lips. She glanced at me and her grin slipped. In a room full of people, there was nothing I could say to her. Instead, I approached her, set my hand on her shoulder and let it rest there. A moment later, she reached up to cover my hand with hers.

"Barrett! I lost your three children!" a blonde, statuesque woman called as she appeared through the back door of the kitchen, a sleeping baby at her shoulder. "They're slippery."

Barrett laughed. "Thanks for watching them last night." She immediately went to greet her friend and brushed a finger across the baby's cheek. "How can he sleep through this?"

"He's a Scot," the woman said with a smile.

"Is your husband behind you?"

"I am," came a gravelly voice. The burly man held a toddler to his hip who looked exactly like her mother.

Barrett brushed her cheek against his in greeting and then leaned over to greet the baby who squealed.

"Oh, so now Carys is a gem," the woman muttered with a roll of her eyes. She went to the cupboard and pulled out two coffee mugs. "She was a beast earlier."

"Where's Da?" Hawk asked.

"On the phone. He'll be down in a minute. You want to say hello to our guests?"

The three boys stopped in their tracks and swiveled their heads toward Quinn and me. The twins had been too young to truly remember how I used to look. Hawk, though, who was almost five, remembered me.

"What's wrong with his face?" Hawk asked.

Kids. So brutal it was like a serrated knife to the ribs.

Three pairs of curious children eyes peered at me. The adults looked at each other, unsure of how to handle it. Except for Quinn.

"He was in an accident," Quinn said, like she was speaking to an adult and not a child.

"Did it hurt?" Iain asked, not wanting to be left out of the inquisition.

"It did," I said.

"Come here," Quinn said, waving at the three boys. "Sasha, sit down."

"Yes, ma'am," I murmured.

She sent me a teasing grin. It was so very Quinn of old that it made my heart swell.

I sat.

The boys came over, slowly, unsure.

"You want to touch his face?" Quinn asked.

"What's it feel like?" Noah wondered, sounding far too articulate for a boy just over four.

"A little rough," she said. "But still like a face. You can compare, if you want."

Hawk climbed up onto her lap first—the devil—and placed his hand on her cheek. "Smooth."

She nodded and then gestured with her eyes to me. I leaned over and Hawk placed his other hand on my face.

"See?" Quinn asked softly. "Not that different."

"Very different," I stated. "You're prettier than I am. Isn't she, Hawk?"

"Very pretty," Hawk agreed, causing Quinn to laugh.

And just like that, the adults started talking again, and Noah and Iain came over to touch my face. My eyes drifted to Quinn's.

There weren't enough words to convey my gratitude. She still saw me as whole. And she made other people see me that way, too.

"What's going on in here?" Campbell demanded from the corner of the kitchen.

Hawk jumped down off Quinn's lap and ran to his father. He wrapped his arms around Campbell's legs and looked up at him. "Uncle Sasha is back!" With a look over his shoulder at me, he demanded, "Did you bring me a present?"

Chapter 17
QUINN

Watching Sasha with Barrett's children over breakfast had my heart fluttering into my throat. I hadn't planned on telling him I was carrying Ori's baby so soon. I hadn't confirmed it, but I remembered what it had been like with Ciaran. I'd had symptoms early.

Did I want Sasha?

Very much.

Did I want this baby?

More than I could express with words.

Maybe I would've felt differently if Ori had been brutal, a monster that wanted to destroy me. But he hadn't shown me any of that. Not until the end, when it came out about why he'd really wanted me.

Brandon had eventually woken up and come downstairs. After flipping the boys over his shoulders like sacks of potatoes, he set them down, grabbed a cup of coffee, and then went to join the men in the library. The boys went upstairs to their playroom and the baby was napping in the nursery.

Barrett bounced Ash's daughter on her knee while they

talked. Every now and again one of them would ask me a question, and then have to repeat it, because I was trapped in my own head.

"When did this turn into a 1950s party?" Ash demanded, standing up from the table. "The men are in one place; we're in the kitchen. I object."

"Cut me another slice of coffee cake, will you?" Barrett asked her best friend.

"Sure thing," Ash said. "Think they're telling off-color jokes?"

"Definitely," Barrett said with a wry grin. "Or you know. Discussing business."

"We could be part of that business discussion," Ash said. She grasped the knife and then decided it wasn't worth it, so she picked up the coffee cake and brought it to the kitchen table. "Let's be real. We're going to eat this entire thing."

"Damn straight," Barrett agreed. She broke a small piece and gave it to Carys. "God, she makes me want another one."

Ash snorted. "You can have her."

Barrett laughed. "She's perfect."

"She's on her best behavior. This is how she lures you in. I swear she's a changeling—definitely Duncan's daughter. She's a heathen." Ash chuckled. "You really want another one?"

"The idea of one," Barrett relented. "Maybe an actual one. I'd love a girl. But we got Flynn fixed."

Ash's laugh was charming and effortless. A perfect blend of socialite and genuine caring. "He's not a dog."

"You're right." Barrett waggled her eyebrows. "He's a beast."

They giggled like two schoolgirls, and then their attention turned to me.

"How are you, Quinn?" Ash asked softly. "You've been quiet."

I shrugged and took a sip of my tea. "Processing everything, I guess."

Ash's eyes darted to Barrett. Barrett nodded. "Are you in love with Sasha?"

"Um. How about a little warm up before the tough questions?"

Ash smiled. "It's not a tough question, not really."

"You condone this line of questioning?" I looked at Barrett, amusement stamped across my lips. It felt good to be in the presence of women, strong women, women who'd married men with questionable morals but unwavering loyalty to their cause and their families.

"I condone and support," Barrett said. "Answer the question, I'm dying to know."

My mouth softened, and my body slackened. I wanted nothing more than to curl up in bed with Sasha, trace the lines of his body with my fingers and mouth. To relearn how we'd once fit together. How we'd fit together again. If we even could.

I wasn't naïve. It would've been hard enough if it had just been Ori between us.

"She loves him," Ash said. "Look at her face."

"Is reconciliation in the future?"

"I—maybe. Yes." I sighed. "It's all sorts of fucked up."

"Because you're married?" Ash pressed.

"When did you get so blunt?" I asked her. "I don't remember you being this blunt."

"I've been married to a Scot for years. My best friend is married to a Scot. I live in *Scotland*. There are Scots and sheep."

"What do sheep have to do with anything?" I asked with a smile.

"I'm not sure," she admitted. "I think it's the pregnancy brain talking."

Silence fell.

"Pregnant?" Barrett asked. "You sure?"

Ash nodded. "Confirmed this morning." She smiled. "Something about the Scottish air. I swear every woman who marries a Scot becomes some sort of fertility goddess."

"Didn't I tell you breast feeding wasn't a good form of birth control?"

"Relax. This one was planned. And it will be my last. I swear."

Barrett let out a shriek of happiness. Carys wiggled off of Barrett's lap, wanting to get away from the noise and then ran out of the room.

A moment later, I heard the sound of the library door open, and the men rushed into the kitchen, looking around like they expected to see a weapon-toting villain.

"What the hell was that noise?" Flynn asked.

"Your wife," Ash said with a laugh.

"Banshee," he muttered. "What's all the fuss about?"

"I just told her I was pregnant, and she flew off the deep end," Ash said.

Hugs and kisses were passed around the room. Before I knew it, Sasha was wrapping his arms around me. I gave into his strength and leaned back against him. He brushed his lips against my ear, and I shivered.

He held me tighter.

Flynn said something in Gaelic, and then Duncan answered with a laugh. Barrett snorted and rolled her eyes.

"What did he say?" I asked.

"They were talking about sperm and virility," she explained. "I'll spare you the actual translation."

Duncan draped his arm around his wife and pulled her

into his side. He whispered something to her, causing her to laugh again.

"You guys are all so sickening," Brandon said with a knowing smirk.

"Jealous?" Flynn asked.

"Not even a little bit. If you'll excuse me, I want to go hang out with the children. They're more fun than you."

"Where's Carys?" Duncan asked.

"She was terrified by Barrett's enthusiasm, and she ran out of here," Ash said. "But I don't know—"

"I'll find her," Brandon promised and left the kitchen.

"Is it too early for a celebratory Scotch?" Flynn asked. "For those that can?"

"Yes," I voiced, not wanting to have to reject the drink and lie. "It's too early."

Flynn frowned. "As soon as the sun sets, we are getting—"

His phone rang, cutting him off. He pulled it out of his trouser pocket. Frowning, he looked at the name flashing across the screen.

"Who is it?" Barrett asked.

"It's Colt. I've got to take this."

Chapter 18
QUINN

As soon as Flynn left the room, Barrett's cell phone rang. It rested on the counter, and she picked it up. "What the hell?"

Everyone fell silent.

She pressed a button. "Hello?" She closed her eyes and pinched the bridge of her nose. "Okay. Yeah." She paused. "He's talking to Colt now. Right. Okay. No we'll take ours. Talk to you in a few."

Barrett hung up, and we all waited for her to tell us what was going on, but she clamped her lips shut and set her phone down.

"Barrett?" Duncan asked.

She shook her head. "Your brother is fine."

"Good," Duncan said with a labored sigh.

"What's going on?" Sasha asked.

"I have to talk to Flynn," she said and left the room.

We looked at Duncan for an explanation. He sighed. "My brother—Ramsey—is in Dallas."

"Why?" I asked.

"Let's sit. It's a long and strange explanation."

We all moved to the table and sat. Duncan held Ash's hand while he talked. "You know about Barrett's association with Mateo Sanchez. And how we package his product in our bottles of Scotch?"

Glorified drug mules, but I didn't say that. Instead I nodded. So did Sasha.

"Well, Ramsey's on the ground and he oversees distribution in the southwest."

"Who's Colt?" Sasha wondered.

"A friend of ours. From when we were young. All of our fathers were friends. SINS members. Colt is President of a motorcycle club in Waco. He's been having some trouble with a rival club—a rival club that has partnered with a Mexican cartel. Colt needs backup."

"And Sanchez will give him the backup if he distributes. Do I have that right?" Sasha asked, making the connection quickly. Faster than I could.

"Exactly." Duncan nodded. "There's also a woman involved... She attracted the notice of the rival president. Colt promised to protect her."

"So why are we worried about Ramsey?" I asked. I liked Duncan's younger brother. He was a lot like Brandon. Charming. Playboy. But a couple of years ago he'd had his heart and trust broken by a young Englishwoman of noble birth, a legit aristocrat. He hadn't been the same since. Reckless, was the word Barrett associated with him.

"He'll want in on the fight," Duncan said. "The lad can't help himself. I'm just afraid because his head is not screwed on properly that he'll get hurt. Or killed."

"Are you going to have to go to Waco?" Ash asked him.

Duncan shook his head. "No. Flynn and Barrett will go. They'll straighten it out. Sanchez would much rather deal with Barrett than any of us, anyway."

EMMA SLATE

I snorted in amusement. Only Barrett. Friends with the most infamous drug lord in Argentina.

"What?" Sasha asked with a raised eyebrow.

"She's got such an interesting group of friends," I said.

"She does," Sasha agreed. With a look at Duncan, he said, "Angelo, too."

"No," Duncan said. "Really?"

Sasha nodded. "I wish I could tell you the entire story, but you know The White Company."

And once again, I was an outsider.

Sasha and Barrett had gone into the lion's den, bartered something of value to The White Company who were nothing more than expensive Italian mercenaries, around since the crusade era. Not a lot was known about them. They valued privacy, and no one spoke of their trials, their blood payments.

"Secrecy is stupid," Ash said.

I snorted out a laugh. "Gossip whore."

She grinned. "Damn right!"

"Secrets don't stay secrets when you tell other people," Sasha pointed out, with a look in my direction.

I clammed up immediately. My secret wouldn't be a secret forever. Eventually, my body would start showing. I just hoped it happened long after Ori was no longer in the picture.

"You're no fun," Ash pouted.

Sasha shrugged. "Your wife doesn't understand, after all these years, does she?"

"Don't talk about me like I'm not here!" she yelled. She picked up a piece of coffee cake and chucked it at him. I ducked because her aim was terrible. It hit my shoulder, broke off into two pieces, and landed on the floor.

"Defiler of coffee cake," I stated, reaching down to pick it up.

Before Ash could make a smart retort, Flynn and Barrett came back into the kitchen.

"Well?" Duncan asked.

"It's escalating in Waco," Flynn said. "We're going to fly out today."

"We?" Ash pressed.

"I'm going, too." Barrett looked at Sasha and then at me. "Are you—This is time sensitive. According to Colt, Mateo is being unreasonable with some of his demands."

"And Barrett thinks she can control that Argentinian Don Juan," Flynn interjected.

"He offered to send his jet for us," she reminded him.

"I want to punch his teeth in," Flynn gritted.

Barrett rolled her eyes. "Boys are ridiculous. I'm so glad we have three of them."

"Are you packed?" he demanded.

"I'm always packed. When was the last time we spent more than a day at home?"

"Valid point, hen." Flynn looked at Sasha. "You need anything, you call. Got it?"

Sasha nodded. "*Da*."

"Let's go say goodbye to the boys," Barrett said.

"I guess that means they're crashing with us for the foreseeable future?" Ash wondered.

"Do you mind?" Barrett asked.

"Nope. But you're going to have to return the favor at some point."

Barrett grinned. "Thank God for nannies."

Chapter 19
QUINN

"What am I supposed to do?" I asked quietly. I didn't want to alert Ash and Duncan, but it didn't seem to matter since they were also speaking in hushed tones, completely absorbed in one another.

"What do you mean?" Sasha bent his head toward me so he could hear me better.

"I mean, Barrett and Flynn are leaving. Where am I supposed to go?"

"First of all," Sasha began, "it's not just you. It's *us.*" He pinned me with a stare. "Okay?"

I nodded. "Okay."

"And for the time being, we're staying right here. Boston isn't safe for you right now. And the bastard is expecting us to show up in New York."

"So I'm just supposed to sit here…and wait?"

"Do you have any other ideas?"

I opened my mouth to snap out a retort, only to realize I didn't have one.

"That's what I thought."

"O'Malley Properties. I need to talk to Harrison. I need a cell phone."

Sasha nodded. "Yeah, you do."

I was itching to do something. Even though Dornoch was the safest place for me at the moment, the idea of sitting around and waiting for all the chips to fall was making me stir crazy.

Ori wouldn't come here. He wouldn't storm an actual castle. He wasn't a fool.

"He won't come here," Sasha said, mirroring what I'd been thinking. "He has a plan for how he wants this to play out. He's been waiting years to make his move. Everything he does is deliberate, with purpose."

My mouth flattened into a line. "That's what terrifies me. We know his motivation, but as far as how he's going to carry it out?"

"Let's go into the library, okay?"

I nodded and stood.

"Where are you guys going?" Duncan asked.

"We need some time alone," Sasha stated.

"Oh really?" Ash asked with a knowing grin.

"Not that kind of alone time," I said. "Like we'd really do that with you guys in the house. Not to mention all this other crap hanging over our heads."

"There's always time for alone time," Duncan stated. He sent his wife a heated look. "Right, love?"

"Brandon was right. You guys are nauseating," I said with a teasing grin.

"To be fair, he said that about all of us," Ash reminded me.

Sasha grasped my hand and led me out of the kitchen and into the library. He shut the door. "Now, we won't be disturbed for a while."

"I hate that I can't speak freely in front of them," I said, taking a seat on one of the couches.

"About the baby, you mean?" he asked, sitting next to me. He placed his arm on the back of the cushion, and I leaned into his embrace.

I sighed. "I just think, for now, it's better that they don't know. I don't want to risk Ori finding out, and as you stated earlier, secrets don't stay secrets when you tell people. Even people you trust."

"No one will hear it from me. I swear."

Setting my hand on his thigh was completely instinctual. "Are you really okay with this? I fell asleep to you looking defeated and broken. Six hours later, you'd reconciled it. I just wanted to make sure… I'm giving you an out. If you want it."

"Look at me, Quinn."

I lifted my head from his chest and stared up at him. "While you were sleeping, I wasn't. I was awake. I thought about it all. Every avenue. Wondering about how things could be between us. If I stayed, if I left. But I knew I'd come back for you—even if I refused to admit it to anyone. I came to Italy, for you. I'll protect you from him even if you decide you don't want to be with me. Because I love you, Quinn." He gently placed his hand on my belly.

"We almost missed our chance. I won't miss it again."

I leaned up to press my lips to his, a soft, tender gesture. But Sasha refused to let it be soft or tender. He grasped the back of my head and kissed me like a man leaving for war. He kissed me like he'd never see me again.

Pulling my mouth from his, I brushed my lips along the ragged side of his jaw. "You're scared, too," I whispered.

"Yeah. I'm scared."

"Nothing is going to happen to me. Not while you're here."

"Ah, *Myshka*. For once, I'm not worried about you. Ori Marino wants me dead. If he succeeds, it means I don't get a long life with you. I'd rather charge into the fires again than die on you. Leave you alone. Leave you with him."

I swallowed. We'd just found each other again. A unique blending of fragility and resolve. We were finally ready to withstand life's tests, but we controlled nothing. Not the rising and setting of the sun, not the changes of the seasons, and most of all—we couldn't control Ori Marino's burning hatred.

"You have to promise me something," he said quietly.

"Anything."

He inhaled a shaky breath. "If something happens, and you're back with him—out of your control—do whatever you have to do to survive. Tell him about his child. Tell him you love him. Lie and tell him you feel nothing for me. Because if I'm going to die, I need to know he won't break you."

"Sasha," I whispered.

"Promise me, Quinn."

I already felt like I'd been unfaithful to him. From the moment Ori had shared my bed. And now that I was wearing Ori's ring and carrying his child, I felt like I'd betrayed Sasha again.

"I don't know if I can," I said, my voice quivering.

"If you can't do it for you, then promise for the sake of the baby."

I caressed his cheek and tried to catch my breath. "All right, Sasha. All right."

Chapter 20
SASHA

"I need to hit something," I said.

Kilmartin looked up from his phone. "Are you asking me to be a volunteer?"

I cracked my neck. "Want to spar?"

"Fuck yeah." Kilmartin stood up from the kitchen table and followed me. "Should we get Quinn to watch? Place bets on how long it will take for me to kick your ass?"

"Quinn is sleeping. And furthermore, she'd bet on me."

"Why that woman loves you, I'll never know."

I opened the door that led into the dungeon. Or what had once been the dungeon. Barrett and Campbell had it remodeled. From time to time, they still used it as a holding cell. But the main room was sectioned off by bulletproof glass. Very much like a police interrogation room. Past that, there was a smaller area that they'd converted into a training room.

What could I say? There were a lot of alpha males in their lives who needed to burn off testosterone and adrenaline.

Kilmartin and I got into the room and immediately

started to stretch. We each picked up a pair of boxing gloves.

"Do you think—"

"Talk after," I growled. "Now, we spar."

Sparring, contrary to popular belief, was not about beating the hell out of each other. It was about conditioning and form. It was about practice, so that when the time came, and you had to fight hand-to-hand combat, you could. And not just hold your own, but win.

After about forty-five minutes, we stopped.

"You've got a lot of rage," Kilmartin panted. He threw off his boxing gloves and reached for a bottle of water.

"You don't even know," I stated, going for my own. Sweat poured off me. All I wanted was a hot shower and to climb into bed next to Quinn. But I wouldn't take that choice from her—I'd taken far too many from her already. I'd wait until she came to me. I might die of unrequited lust in the process, but so be it.

"I never thought you were good enough for her," Kilmartin said, his voice soft yet full of steel. "Told Michael that on more than one occasion."

"Why wasn't I good enough? Because I was a poor Russian immigrant who killed his way to the top?"

Kilmartin shook his head. "Self-made man. I respect that. My parents live a modest life. Not like this." He gestured to the sparring room. "I was just beginning to like you, and then you walked away. So I hated you all over again."

"I'm back now. I'm making it right."

He nodded thoughtfully. "Maybe."

"That's not for you to say. This is between Quinn and me."

Kilmartin looked up from his bottle of water to stare at me with eyes glittering with resignation.

"You're in love with her," I said.

"I—"

"You should've been in Boston with her. The moment I was gone, you should've gotten your ass on a plane and stood by her side. Been the shoulder she cried on. She would've fallen in love with you instead of that fucking bastard."

Kilmartin started. "She's not in love with Marino."

I lifted my gaze to the gray ceiling. "Of course she is."

"But how can she—if she loves you."

"Your naïveté is amusing." I let out a mirthless chuckle.

"Don't patronize me. Explain it to me."

I cocked my head to one side. "You know when you break up with a woman and you're getting over her? Then you meet someone new. But there's this…in between period. Where you love the person from your past, but you're falling for the person you're with. It's kind of like that."

"Kind of?"

"Loving two people at once, really loving them, that conflicted feeling…you ever feel that?"

"No."

"Be glad."

He fell silent for a moment and then asked, "How do you know she loves him? Did she tell you?"

"She didn't have to." I sighed and sat down on a bench along the wall, stretching out my legs. "When I left her"— the words physically hurt me to say—"I left her open. Vulnerable, needy. She had no one. He got to her."

"How can she love him already? It's been what? A few weeks? A month?"

"Aside from the extenuating circumstances? She was alone. She had no memories. Whatever he told her, she believed. And the thing is, any lies he spun, they reached into the heart of her and made her fall for him. Besides, Quinn doesn't fall in love easily, but when she does, it's fast. Fast, honest, raw. That's all Quinn."

Kilmartin adjusted his stance and looked down at the ground. "I wanted to go to Michael's funeral. She told me not to come and jeopardize my safety. I'm … wanted in the States." He paused. "Safety be damned. I should've gone."

He walked around the training room and then looked at me. "You would've gone. No matter what."

It gutted me to hear that he'd known about Michael O'Malley's death, and he didn't attend the wake. I would've gone. I would've paid my respects, stood by Quinn's side, even if she hadn't wanted me there.

But I hadn't known.

"You're not good enough for her," he said softly. "But she wants you anyway."

"Thank Christ she does," I said, my voice strained. "Because I don't know what I'd do without her."

Chapter 21
QUINN

I woke up to darkness. I'd gone to sleep when it was still light out, but now moonlight peeked through the curtains of the guest room. I lay there for a moment, contemplating moving, contemplating everything else that swirled around in my head.

My emotions were not my own.

I was pregnant.

But not with Sasha's baby.

I cried for that. I cried for myself and the situation I was in. I was stupid and naïve. I'd fallen for lies, as golden and as warm as the sun. I'd been cold for so long.

Ori Marino was a sociopath.

He'd played the part. Charming, understanding, sensual.

God, so sensual.

Even now, the thought of him made me quiver.

I hated myself for that, too.

He was beautiful. Seductive. An angel's face hiding a dark demonic soul.

He'd cut off his own cousin's finger. He'd presented it to me like the huntsman presented the deer heart to the evil queen.

He'd caressed me and made love to me. He'd kissed away the scars on my belly. He'd held me while I cried for another man—the man who'd killed his best friend.

My hand went to my stomach.

I carried his child.

What would he do if he found out?

He couldn't know. He could never know.

I understood why Sasha made me promise to do what I had to do to survive. Ori Marino had wanted me. But want wasn't love. The term "crime of passion" had been invented for him. He'd punish me. For leaving him, betraying him, for choosing Sasha.

If I ever found myself in his clutches again…

The door to the bedroom opened. It was a soft sound, and if I'd been asleep, it wouldn't have even woken me.

I rolled over and switched on the lamp. Sasha's features were garish in the golden light.

"Did I wake you?" he asked.

"No. I was up."

He shut the door and then came to the bed. I scooted over to give him room. He kicked off his shoes and then climbed in next to me.

"Can I ask you something?" I nuzzled against his side and rested my face on his chest.

"You can ask me anything.

I paused before blurting out, "Why do you love me?"

"What?"

"I mean—why do you love me? I'm weak and I need to be taken care of. I'm superficial and pampered. Why do you love me, Sasha?"

"When you say *weak*, do you mean physically?"

"I'm"—I inhaled—"I'm not like Barrett. I can't fight like her. And I am weak mentally, too. A stronger person would've seen past his facade."

"Sit up," he commanded. "I need you to see my face when I say what I'm going to say."

Swallowing, I slowly sat up and faced him, pulling my legs up to my chest and wrapping my arms around my knees.

"First of all," he said. "Barrett is Barrett and you are Quinn. Everyone is different. She's different. Dolinsky changed her, okay? If that hadn't happened, I wonder how she would be. Scottish historian in love with Campbell. But that situation turned her into someone she wasn't.

"You're not mentally weak either. Look at all you went through. Your mother passed away. Your father passed away. You and I…and the baby. You're not weak. You're the strongest woman I know. So don't you fucking blame yourself for believing him. He backed up his words with actions—and you have nothing to be ashamed about. Okay?"

"Okay," I whispered.

"As for you being superficial and pampered? Maybe you were as a teen. But you grew out of that. A superficial woman wouldn't have stayed by my side and loved me even after the fire. But you stayed. And you never made me feel like less. God, you're so good and strong. So I need you to stop thinking of yourself as weak. Not all warriors carry guns, but you're a warrior through and through."

His eyes pinned me with intensity. When he reached for me, I moved away. "Wait," I said. "I need to show you something."

I climbed off the bed. I pulled the sweats down,

enough to reveal my belly, and then lifted my shirt. "Can you see them?" I whispered.

Sasha peered at my stomach. "I want to turn on the main light."

I nodded and he got off the bed. He hit the light switch on the wall. The room brightened, and I swallowed in fear. There was no hiding now.

He came back to the bed and sat down, his legs over the edge. He grasped my hips and pulled me to him. His fingers traced the lines of my body, gently, cautiously.

"What did it feel like?" he asked, his voice quiet.

"Weird," I said with a strangled laugh. "Like your body isn't your own, and then one day your stomach just…pops. And there's a baby in there, and you're never just you again."

"I'm so damn sorry." It was hard for him to get the words through his throat. He leaned over and brushed his lips against my skin. "I'm sorry I left. I'm sorry you suffered alone."

I stroked my hand against the close-cropped hair on his head. "We both have scars, don't we?"

He nodded and lifted his blue eyes to mine. They held a world of pain. Regret and remorse.

"Stop punishing yourself," I said. "We don't stand a chance in hell if you keep thinking you'll never make it up to me."

He leaned over and pressed his cheek to my breastbone. "Quinn…"

"I sometimes think I should've left you first. You told me often enough. Those first few months after the accident. We might've turned out differently."

"You refused to listen. Stubborn woman."

"I couldn't bear the thought of leaving you."

"I didn't want to leave you, Quinn. I swear. I just… I

was nearly out of my head, and I don't know if there's any explanation that will make it okay."

My hand moved down to his neck, which I started to massage. "Would you have left Barrett? If you'd been together?"

He looked up at me. "Is it always going to come back to her?"

I thought for a moment and shook my head. "No. It's not even about her, really. She's just the yardstick by which I judge myself."

"And my love for you?" He sighed. "I don't love you like I love her. And I didn't even think about if I would've left her if we'd been together because we weren't together. We haven't been together. We're never going to be together." His eyes searched mine. "A man in his right mind would never leave you. Not by choice."

"You had a choice."

"Not really." He licked his lips and looked pensive. "How can I explain? Let's say I didn't leave. Let's say our relationship turned into this thing of you taking care of me. Even after I was up and moving around, you were still taking care of me—emotionally. You talk about being fragile? No. You're iron. You held me up when I couldn't do it for myself."

"So I made you feel ashamed? Less than a man? Just by loving you?"

"Who was taking care of *you*?" he demanded. "Because it wasn't me. I couldn't take care of myself. And you were taking care of me, so who took care of you?"

"There are times in relationships when it has to be all about the other person. Maybe not forever, but it ebbs and flows. You took care of me before I took care of you."

His mouth tightened. "Did you stay by my bedside out of obligation?"

I thought for a moment. "No. I stayed for love."

"Love and obligation go hand in hand. Look at family dynamics."

"I don't know, Sasha. I stayed because I loved you. Because I had hope that we'd get back to some sort of normal. Maybe we'd never be what we once were, but I knew we'd find our new normal. In time."

I looked over his head to stare at the wall. "Barrett warned me. That you weren't going to be the same if you lived through the burns. I thought I heard her. I thought I understood, but I guess I didn't."

"I didn't even know who I was going to be if I lived," he pointed out. "Which is why I had to leave. I had to leave so I could discover me again. So I wouldn't resent you or wonder if you stayed with me out of obligation."

"Resent me? Why would you resent me?"

He smiled. "Because you were so damn selfless. And I couldn't—I didn't know if I was ever going to be whole again. And I didn't want a cheerleader. I wanted a partner, yet I couldn't even be that for you, and I wasn't sure I could be that for you ever again."

I ran my finger across his scarred cheek and then over his right eyebrow. "You know what people see when they look at you?"

"An ugly bastard."

I didn't laugh at his attempt at self-deprecation. "They see scars, they see flaws, they see brokenness. You know what I see? A man willing to charge into the flames for me. You're beautiful, you're perfect, you're everything I could've hoped for."

One of his hands slipped down my hipbone, slowly journeying toward the crevice between my thighs. "Do you still want me? Here?" He gently pressed the heel of his hand against my cleft.

Desire hit me low and fast. I inhaled sharply. My thumbs skated along his jaw. I forced him to look up at me, and I smiled.

"That was never our problem, was it?"

"Do you want me, Quinn?"

I leaned down and pressed my lips to his. "I want you. Scars and all."

Chapter 22

QUINN

We left the bedroom and took the stairs slowly. I gripped his hand tighter, wanting to convey the strength of our intimacy through our simple touch. Sasha's hand squeezed mine, telling me he understood.

"Did Barrett and Flynn leave?" I asked.

"Yes. They didn't want to wake you."

"I don't feel like I've slept nearly enough."

"Adrenaline."

"Yeah." And the fact that I was pregnant. Which still threw me for a loop.

"Do you want to get out of the house for a little while?" he asked, jarring me out of my own thoughts. "Maybe go into town. Have dinner? Pretend everything is completely normal."

"I don't have clothes of my own," I said.

"You and Ash are about the same size," he said. "I'm sure you could borrow from her if you want. Barrett also has accounts with all the boutiques in Dornoch You could put some clothes on her tab."

I shook my head. "It's weird not having access to my

own things. My own money. Which reminds me, I've really put off calling people long enough."

"Use the phone in Flynn's study. It's a safe line."

Nodding, I dropped his hand. "I'm not in the mood to go out. Is that okay?"

He smiled and pressed a kiss to my lips. "It's more than okay. Ash and Duncan took the kids for the night. So we have the house to ourselves."

"What about Brandon?"

"He—ah—left."

I blinked. "He didn't wait to say goodbye? What did he have to get home to?"

Sasha rubbed the back of his neck.

"What aren't you telling me?" I demanded.

"He and I—we sparred while you were asleep."

"Did you beat the crap out of him? And now his ego is bruised?"

He shook his head. "No. Nothing like that. He just... He's in love with you."

I scoffed. "Brandon? No."

"Trust me."

"You guys talked about me?"

"It wasn't like that," he said.

I placed my hands on my hips. "What was it like then?"

"Two guys in love with the same girl making peace with each other. And let's talk about why you don't believe me when I tell you he's in love with you."

"Because it's Brandon."

"That's not an explanation."

"It's—We've known each other for years. He flirted and teased, but I never once thought he felt anything stronger for me than friendship."

He rolled his eyes. "He came to Italy. For you."

"No. He came because Flynn couldn't come. Otherwise it would've been you, Flynn, and Barrett in charge of that mission."

Sasha laughed and then wrapped his arms around me.

"What? Why are you laughing at me," I demanded, feeling a tug of amusement at the corners of my lips.

"Because despite you being so worldly, you're still so naïve."

"Naïve is bad. Naïve gets you into trouble."

"You were sheltered, Quinn."

"Too sheltered." I shook my head. "Dad left me his company with no instructions. Just an apology."

"You don't need instructions."

"On how to apply lip liner? Yeah, you're right. I nail that every time. On how to run a billion-dollar company that fell into my lap? Different story. A roadmap would've been really helpful."

He guided me toward Flynn's study. "How were you doing with it?"

"Before I got derailed?" I thought a moment. "I think I was finding my way. It was challenging, but I'd needed a challenge. And a distraction."

"And that's why your father didn't leave you any instructions. He knew you'd figure it out, and he knew you'd do it in your own way."

I looked at him and shook my head. "I can't believe I forgot."

"Forgot what?"

"That you have a way of seeing things that makes total sense. I've missed it. I've missed you."

He cradled my cheek in his hand and stared at me like I was the only woman he ever saw. The future was in his eyes—we just had to get through the present.

I absentmindedly fiddled with the rings on my left hand. Crushing, paralyzing fear overwhelmed me. I took a step back, needing a moment away from him. Sasha was all encompassing, and I tended to forget myself when I was around him. It was easy to let him take care of me, to fall into the trap of letting a man handle it all.

I was tired of being the woman who relied on men— and when they left or died—I had to pick up the pieces. I shouldn't have to pick up the pieces.

"Quinn?"

I shook my head. "I just need some time…to catch my breath. To think. I haven't had time to think, ya know?"

He was frowning when I finally looked at him. "All right. I'll be in the library."

"I'll find you after I make some calls."

Sasha almost reached out to touch me, but then he thought better of it, and his hand dropped to his side. He strode away down the hall. I watched him go, disappearing into the library.

I turned and entered Flynn's study, determined to get out of my own mess.

Chapter 23
SASHA

I knew she was running scared. Once the adrenaline wore off, once she realized she was safe, Quinn came back to herself. Now she was retreating. Hiding from me, pushing me away, keeping me at arm's length.

She hadn't processed everything. Not the baby, not her marriage, not the fact that I said I didn't care that the baby wasn't mine.

It was mine.

I claimed it as my own.

I would love it as my own.

My cell phone rang. With a weary sigh, I answered Dimitri's call. "Well, we have a bit of a problem."

"Don't we always," I said dryly.

"The Marino restaurant burned to the ground."

I sat up straight. "Excuse me?"

"Three days ago."

"Convenient. The Marinos did it themselves?"

"Or paid people to do it."

Why would they burn a profitable restaurant to the ground? Mama Marino's restaurant had been a successful enterprise for over twenty years. It was a meeting place, and the aging Italian bosses went there to conduct business. It was a staple in the Italian Mafioso world.

"How much was the insurance on that place?" I asked.

Dimitri said a sizeable number. "Here's the thing, though. They held the same policy for years, but a few months ago, it increased."

"What does Ori Marino need traceable money for?" I wondered. "He's an Italian boss."

"I'm not sure yet. No one is talking. There's not even a whisper of the Marino name in this neighborhood. It's like…"

"What?" I demanded. I was impatient, and now this thing with Quinn had me on edge.

"It's like the neighborhood remembers. They remember what they lost. Marino Sr. dying changed everything, but they adapted because they had to. Marino Jr. dying sent them into another tailspin. Ori Marino disappeared after the death of his father and brother."

"Where did he go?"

"I have no idea. No one does. That restaurant and Mama Marino were all that were left to hold the tattered neighborhood together. There wasn't another leader among them, Sasha."

"Mama Marino," I said softly. "That's what everyone calls her."

It's what I had called her when I'd sat at her tables with Igor. Igor who had felt safe and comfortable among the Italians. He'd considered them family. They'd considered him family.

They'd never been my family. I'd found a different one —my loyalty had changed when I met Barrett. And what I'd wanted for my boys had changed too.

"What are you thinking about? You've gone quiet," Dimitri noted.

"I just wonder why alliances change. Igor did business with the Italians. Now we do business with the Scots." I couldn't imagine a time when Barrett and I were no longer friends, when her husband wasn't a close friend of mine and didn't want to be linked any longer.

What did it take to cut the strings of friendship?

Monarchs of Europe used to marry off their sons and daughters to form alliances. Powerful, political families were no different. But Igor had started his own trend and married for love.

Barrett had married for love.

I was going to marry for love.

The only one who hadn't married for love was Ori Marino.

The world was changing—our worlds were changing.

I thought of Barrett and Campbell's children. Who would they marry?

"Sasha?" Dimitri pressed. "What do you want me to do?"

"Keep digging," I stated. I couldn't see the big picture yet. There were pieces missing. I just hoped when I discovered them, it wouldn't be too late.

Dimitri paused and then said, "Yeah. Okay."

"We need to follow that money trail. Find the insurance agent that increased the policy amount and find out what Marino did with the money he collected. There has to be a witness to someone setting the fire. None of that shit happens without at least one street bum watching."

"All right, Sasha, all right."

"And sometimes, it's not about violence or money. It's about offering someone something they really need."

"What the hell does that mean? Who doesn't want money? Who doesn't respond to violence?"

I rubbed my forehead, feeling the start of a headache coming on. Exhaustion and stress did that to a person. Maybe I was becoming delirious, and my thoughts were cloudy.

"Sometimes all you have to do is offer a cup of coffee or a smile. People will talk if they think you don't want anything from them."

"We all want something from someone. Maybe you should be the one to do this. You seem to know what you're after, what information you're trying to find."

"My face is memorable. Yours is not."

"Are you saying I'm completely generic looking?"

"I'm saying you're handsome, and when you smile you look like you're in a gum commercial."

"Ah, I didn't know you felt that way."

"Shut up," I said on a laugh. "You know what I mean."

"What you should've said was 'Damn, Dimitri, you are one hot piece of—'"

"And we're done here."

"It's good to hear you laugh, brother," he said, the teasing fading from his tone. "Damn good."

"Feels good," I admitted.

"All because of Quinn? Never mind, I already know the answer. There's hope for you then."

"Unless Ori Marino gets his way and turns me into Russian sausage."

"It'll never come to that. We won't let it."

"Some things are out of our control."

"Who are you?" he wondered. "You were the man who once controlled everything."

I looked into the fireplace. The coals from last night's

fire were still warm. It wouldn't take a lot to stoke them into a new blaze.

"I was burned in a fire. I should've died." I paused. "We control nothing. Not enough money and power to cheat death. Death has no allegiance."

"You're not dead yet," he pointed out.

"Let's keep it that way, *da*?"

"*Da*," he agreed.

Chapter 24

QUINN

"You sure you're okay, lass?" came Donovan's gruff voice.

"I'm safe," I said to the man I considered an uncle.

"That's not really what I meant. Though I'm relieved to hear it."

I sighed. "I'm…okay. I guess."

"I'm glad to hear your voice. That Russian of yours sent his men to watch my back. Call them off."

"It's for your own good," I said. "Ori might hurt you to get to me."

The craggy Irishman snorted. "I can handle that Italian Lothario."

"Do people really use that word anymore?" I asked with a chuckle.

"I do."

"Showing your age there, you know."

"Hush, you," he growled. "Let me talk."

"So talk."

"You need to come back to Boston immediately."

"I can't. You know I can't. It's not safe for me there—"

"He's taken over O'Malley Properties."

"What?"

"Ori. He's here in Boston, and he's taken control of your father's company."

"But, how?" I demanded in shock. "How can he do that?"

"You married him, didn't you?"

"I—It won't stick. On grounds that I wasn't of sound mind."

"Well, until that goes into effect, he's running O'Malley Properties. Walked right in, sat behind your father's desk, and took over. Harrison called him on it. Marino showed him a piece of paper that looks like your signature stating you gave him control."

"I didn't sign anything. It's forged; it's bullshit."

"Did you sign a prenup, Quinn?"

"No," I whispered.

"What the ever-loving fuck," he snapped.

"I had amnesia," I said, my voice weak. It was all so stupid. I was stupid. I'd lost my memory and believed Ori when he told me we were engaged, told me we were building a life."

"Get on the phone with your lawyer right now. Start divorce proceedings. Block his claim. Something."

I didn't tell Donovan that Sasha had plans to make me a widow. No doubt Donovan would volunteer to help.

"This has to stay quiet," I stated, getting back to the matter at hand. "If word gets out that I—O'Malley Properties is done. No one is going to want to do business with me. Ever. I need to call Dave Flannigan. He said if I ever needed anything…"

"What can I do?" he asked.

"Call the mayor. Call the police chief. Call all of my father's old friends and tell them it's not true. That I'm suffering from an internal hostile takeover—or whatever the jargon is."

"I will."

"I'll be getting a new cell phone. I'll call you with the new number."

"If I need to get a hold of you, how am I supposed to do that?"

"Hold on." I set the phone down and rushed to the door. I threw it open and hustled toward the library. As I got to the sliding doors, they parted, and Sasha stepped out.

"What's wrong?" he asked, taking in the pinched worry on my face.

I took his hand and dragged him back to Flynn's study. I picked up the phone. "You there, Donovan?"

"Yeah, I'm here."

"Okay." I looked at Sasha. "He needs a way to reach me. Give him your cell number."

"That's not a good idea," Sasha said.

"I didn't ask if it was a good idea," I snapped, temper fraying. "Give me the number."

He stared at me for a long moment and then rattled off his number. "You got that, Donovan?"

"Got it. I'll be in touch. Don't worry, lass. We won't let him get away with this. Call Flannigan."

"I will." I hung up with him and was just about to dial information. I didn't have Dave Flannigan's card on me anymore, so I had no idea his personal cell number. Hopefully his office would transfer me. But before I could punch a number, Sasha's hand stopped me.

"Tell me what's going on."

"There isn't time for that right now."

His hand tightened around my wrist. "There's always

time. And you look like you're in a full-blown panic. Tell me and I can help."

With a deep breath, I nodded. I dropped the receiver into the cradle and collapsed in the chair behind Flynn's massive desk.

"Ori's in Boston. Apparently, he's attempting to take over O'Malley Properties—or he has. He has a paper claiming I gave him rights to make decisions as president. But I didn't, Sasha. I didn't sign anything! And now the bastard is going to use my father's company to—"

"To get you to step foot in Boston," he finished, his face grim.

"I have to go," I said, desperation coating my tongue. "I can't let him do this. I can't let him take my legacy away from me. I can't let him take more from me."

Sasha placed his hands on the desk and leaned over. "We won't let him get away with this."

"So we'll go to Boston?"

His eyes were fierce, his jaw set. "We'll go to Boston."

"This is a terrible idea."

"The worst," he agreed.

"I have to call my lawyer."

"You should. You want me to stay?"

For the first time in my life, I wanted to handle something all on my own. I wanted to be the bearer of my own consequences.

I rose slowly from the chair. "No. I've got this."

Chapter 25
QUINN

I turned my face up to the shower head and let the hot water beat down on me. After a two-hour phone call with Dave Flannigan, I was exhausted. He was filing an injunction to stop Ori, but he said it was all for show. There were things he said he couldn't talk about to me, but that he'd handle it. Back door politics, I guessed.

We were all a bunch of criminals. And I lumped myself in that category now, too. Because even though I wasn't doing anything illegal, I'd stood by long enough and watched those close to me live outside the law.

I hadn't cared how my father made his money, only that I'd had nice things and beautiful clothes. I hadn't cared that his power and influence opened all the doors for me and that I'd felt like I'd owned Boston. No club or restaurant ever turned me away. Everyone had known my name. I'd enjoyed it.

And then I'd met Sasha, and it was an entirely new world brought before my eyes. Manhattan. It was one thing to feel like I was a princess of Boston. But on Sasha's arm, I'd felt like a queen.

He was savage and brutal, as were the men who followed him. Yet they'd shown me none of that brutality. None of the violence had touched me.

Even Ori, when he'd finally shed his golden skin to reveal the snake underneath. He'd had other ways to use his hands to show his true power. He'd taken my desire for him and turned it against me. No, he hadn't needed to slap or hit.

A man who beat a woman wasn't powerful at all. He was a coward.

Ori was no coward.

I shivered and turned the water hotter.

There was a knock on the bathroom door.

"Come in!"

A moment later, I could see Sasha's lazy figure through the opaque glass of the shower door. "Ash brought clothes for you. I put them on the bed."

"Thanks." I closed my eyes and slumped down, letting the water rain over me.

"Quinn? Are you okay?"

"I'm just tired, ya know?" I said, my voice soft. I wondered if he could hear me over the din of the shower, but I didn't have the strength to speak up.

His hand touched the glass, and I reached up to put my hand there, too. Even hazy, his hand was so much bigger than mine. I looked at my fingers. Long, delicate. My mother's hands.

The diamond on my finger was cloudy through the steam. Murky.

"I know what it's like to be tired," he said finally. His hand remained on the glass, like a lifeline. "I know that it feels like it's all coming down around you and just when you catch your breath, something else goes wrong.

"I know it feels like you can't rely on anyone but yourself." His voice had become lower. "I know it feels like you're alone."

"I am alone," I interrupted. Bitter anguish slithered through me, coating my tongue, my words.

"You're not alone. You have me."

"Can you promise me safety? The safety of my friends and family—what's left of them? The safety of my unborn child?"

He fell silent.

"I know you're here. I know I'm not alone, but these are my mistakes to rectify. And I'll be damned if I sit on the sidelines and let a man handle it for me. I need to handle it. It's time I handled it."

"That's not the way—"

"Barrett handles shit all the time," I interrupted. "And don't deny it and tell me it's not true. When she talks, people listen. When she demands something, it gets done. When I say something, all eyes slide to you. Or they looked to my father. Or Ori. Don't you see? I let myself become ineffectual. I let myself be swept aside. I've been an empty-headed trophy my entire adult life. No more."

"What do you want me to do? Teach you to fight? Teach you to fire a weapon? I'll do all those things. I'll do whatever you want."

Is that what I wanted? Would that make me feel powerful? I wanted power in my own right. I wanted to feel in control.

I slowly stood up, careful not to slip.

"Right now? I want you in this shower with me."

He paused. "You sure?"

"Yes."

"If I get in there, I'm going to touch. I'm going to have to touch you." His voice was raw, pleading. "I'm going to need you to touch me too."

I smiled. "I plan on it."

Through the blurred glass, I saw him slip out of his clothes. The shower door opened, and Sasha stepped inside.

It was different now, seeing his naked body. Him seeing mine. We were both scarred, changed.

His hands reached out to immediately stroke the marks on my belly. "You're beautiful," he said quietly, his eyes reverent.

My fingers skated down his right side, starting at the top of his head where the hair had trouble growing, all the way down to his thigh. "So are you."

He snorted.

"No, you are," I insisted. I curled my fist and placed it against his chest, over his heart. "The packaging might've changed a bit, but you're still beautiful. To me."

"I guess that's all that matters then." He leaned down and captured my lips.

I wrapped my arms around his neck, needing to feel his body, needing to feel his skin.

His tongue was inside my mouth, reminding me that sometimes words weren't enough. We were frozen in time, in this moment, as we relearned each other.

Our hands were greedy, our mouths hot. I was desperate and achy. I wanted to cry and scream at the same time. To claw at him and hurt him because he'd hurt me. Yet I wanted to pull him closer and demand he never leave me again.

I wanted to be strong, but my love for Sasha made me weak.

"I need you," I gasped against his mouth when his fingers sought the sliver between my legs.

"I know, *Myshka*, I know."

"Not that way."

"No?" He slid a finger inside of me.

My hands went to his shoulders. I needed something to hold onto. While Sasha pumped his finger into me, he slid his other hand to the back of my thigh.

"Lift," he growled.

I raised my leg and opened myself up to him. My back hit the wall of the shower, and Sasha's finger went deeper.

"You need me?" he asked. "But not this way?"

He remembered how to touch me, how to pleasure me. I stared at him through heavy-lidded eyes. Water made his blond hair darker. It glistened on his skin, turned it red and angry—especially where the skin grafts had been.

"Don't stop," I begged, not caring I was shameless or wearing another man's ring. My heart had always belonged to Sasha. And so had my body.

"You don't need me, Quinn," he stated, guttural and raspy. "You want me. There's a difference."

My hand snaked behind his neck to pull him closer. My lips brushed against his. "I gave you everything. Why couldn't you do the same?"

His finger slid out of me to take himself in hand.

"No," I whispered.

Sasha's face went slack. "No?"

I caressed his cheek. "I want it. I want you. But I'm not ready—" I shook my head and lowered my gaze, even though I had nothing to apologize for. I anticipated a cold draft of air at his departure. I didn't expect to feel his arms come around me, hauling me against his chest.

"We are our choices, Quinn. We have to come to grips with them, look in the mirror and face ourselves. Can you face yourself?"

I thought for a moment. I was embarrassed and angry. At myself and at Ori. But I'd use that. Ori Marino thought

I was just a stupid airhead who needed a man's protection. I couldn't wait to show him whom he'd really married.

"Yeah, Sasha. I can face myself."

He pressed his lips to my shoulder. "The rest will work itself out."

Chapter 26
QUINN

The next morning, I saw the doctor in Dornoch, and she told me I was further along than I'd thought.

"Not possible," I stated.

She smiled. "Possible. For sure."

"But I was using protection up until a couple of weeks ago."

"Condoms?"

I nodded.

"They can fail."

"Yeah, I know that but…" I gasped.

That fucker. That God damn charming Italian prick was the smoothest criminal I'd ever met.

He'd admitted to wanting me pregnant with his child. Trapped. An ultimate fuck you to Sasha.

Ori Marino had poked holes in the condoms. I was sure of it.

"Are you going to tell the father tonight?" the doctor asked with a kind smile, not at all aware of the alarm she'd triggered.

I smiled, wondering if it looked feral. "I'm pretty sure he already knows."

She patted my arm and then left me alone so I could dress.

Any affection I might've harbored for him disappeared. Callous. Manipulative. He'd been playing me since before I'd even met him.

I wanted to choke him with my own two hands.

Did I want him to die?

Was I an evil human being if I said yes?

The men close to me took lives like kids took pennies. It was nothing to them. Not nothing, that wasn't true. But they had no trouble disposing of their enemies. They killed in the name of love, family, and loyalty. Did that make it right? Wasn't my call. I wasn't the final judgment.

But could I pull the trigger myself? Stand in front of Ori Marino, the father of my unborn child, and pull the trigger? Could I watch the life fade from his eyes and not lose any sleep over it?

Doubtful.

What would it cost me if I were the one to end his life? A sleepless night? Many sleepless nights? When my child grew up, would I see glimpses of Ori in him—or her?

As I pulled on my clothes, I thought about what kind of person it would make me if I let Sasha do it. Absolve myself of Ori's death. Sure, I wouldn't be the one to end his life, but give permission to do it? It meant condoning it. It meant being an accomplice.

Sasha greeted me when I came into the waiting room. His smile was wide and pure. Happy. "All right?"

I nodded and brushed my hand across his cheek. "Everything's fine."

His lips grazed my palm. "Good."

He took my hand in his, and we walked out of the doctor's office and into the cold, drizzly day.

"You sure you're okay?" Sasha asked as he steered us in the direction of the car.

I flipped up the collar of my coat. "When are we leaving for Boston?"

"Few hours."

The car was only half a block away, and I hadn't wanted to bother with an umbrella. I jogged the last few feet when I realized the drizzle was about to become a downpour.

We climbed into the car, and Sasha quickly started the engine. Once we were on our way back to Barrett's, I said, "Ori did this on purpose."

"Did what on purpose?"

"Got me pregnant. Tampered with the condoms."

When Sasha remained silent, I pulled my gaze from the scenery outside the window to look at him.

"Why aren't you saying anything?"

He sighed.

"You knew," I accused.

"I suspected," he corrected.

"And you're not mad? Why aren't you mad? And why the hell didn't you tell me you suspected?"

"It wouldn't have changed the outcome"—he glanced at me—"so what was the point? And the last thing you needed was more shit to be upset about."

"So you decided to let me find out on my own? Instead of telling me?" I groaned in frustration. "This is the exact thing I'm talking about. Why does everyone keep things from me? Coddle me?"

"You're pregnant."

"Barrett was pregnant through a lot, and none of you kept anything from her!"

"Barrett is—"

"I swear to God if you say she's different I'm going to punch you in the throat."

Sasha flashed me a smile, and I hated that it diffused my anger. But only temporarily. "He probably already knows then, doesn't he?" I whispered.

"I imagine he suspects, yes."

"It's why you didn't fight me on going back to Boston. You don't think he'll hurt me. Otherwise you wouldn't risk putting me in danger."

He gripped the steering wheel. "I think he really loves you, Quinn. And I think he wants me dead almost as much as he wants you back with him."

I squeezed my eyes closed. "It doesn't matter if he truly loves me or not."

"No?"

"You think I want him," I said. "Still. After everything he's done to me?"

"What did he really do to you? Promise to protect you? Love you? Share a life with you?" Bitterness crossed his face. "He never left you."

"And that should make up for lying to me and knocking me up without my permission?" I snapped. "You're warped if you think I'd want him ever again."

"What's that saying? Thou doth protest too much?"

"What do you think I'm doing, Sasha? Pretending to want you only so that you'll take me back to Boston so he can ambush you?"

"No, I don't think that. I don't think that at all. I know you love me. It's just… I think you love him too."

"I don't."

He fell silent as we continued to drive back to Barrett's house. In a few hours we'd be on a plane to Boston. A few hours were not enough time to decide how I felt about Ori Marino.

Chapter 27

SASHA

Quinn fell asleep a few minutes after takeoff, her head resting on my shoulder. I'd found a small private carrier to fly us into Boston. I paid off the customs officers—Quinn didn't have a passport on her—because the last thing we needed was to alert Marino we were back. At least before we were ready to face him.

The plane dropped through the clouds, and Quinn made a noise in her sleep. I raised my arm to wrap around her, and she immediately snuggled against my chest. She'd have a hell of a crick in her neck if she slept like that for a long time.

I gently lifted her head, and she made a groan of protest. I quickly raised the armrest between us and urged her down so she was lying in my lap. My fingers ran through her hair, and I took comfort in the simple act. I never thought I'd get to hold her in my arms again, let alone touch her while she slept. It was intimate, and it meant she trusted me.

She wondered why I hadn't been angrier at her admission over what Marino had done. The truth was, in his

EMMA SLATE

position, I'd have done the exact same thing. But because Quinn was Quinn and she wanted to believe the best in people, the idea hadn't even crossed her mind.

It had crossed mine, though, and when I knew it was the truth, I'd punched a hole in Barrett's training wall. But then I calmed the fuck down and realized it didn't change how I felt about Quinn, and it didn't change how I felt about ending Marino's life. The only thing it did change was how I viewed him. I knew he cared for her. Because if he didn't, he would've slit her throat and sent me the picture. We would've been in all-out war, but he hadn't done that.

The bastard had fallen in love with her.

And I planned to use that against him.

But how was I going to do that and not put Quinn in danger?

Ori Marino wasn't a better man than me. He was cut from the same vengeful cloth.

I would not sacrifice her for the end game. She would not be a pawn. I wouldn't lose her again.

When we faced one another, it would be just the two of us, our vendettas, our grievances, and everything else that stood between us. Igor's death. My taking over Italian territory.

It needed to end—and it would. When one or both of us was dead.

"Sasha," Quinn whispered.

"What is it, *Myshka?*"

"I'm going to be sick."

She bolted up and put a hand to her mouth. With the other, she fumbled for her seatbelt. When it was clear she wouldn't be able to get it off without help, I quickly reached over and released her. She shot up, nearly fell onto my lap in her haste to get away, and dashed down the aisle.

A moment later, I heard the door to the bathroom slam shut.

"Is she all right?" the flight attendant asked. "Motion sickness?"

I smiled. "Ah, I think something akin to morning sickness."

The woman smiled. "Congratulations."

"Thank you."

"I'll bring her some ginger ale. It'll settle her stomach."

Quinn returned a few minutes later, looking pale. She eased past me and collapsed into her seat.

"You okay?" I placed my hand on her thigh. "The flight attendant is bringing you some ginger ale."

"Thanks," she mumbled. "Fucking great."

"What?"

The flight attendant strolled down the aisle with a plastic cup full of ice and bubbly liquid. "I have some pretzels too. That might help. Your husband told me you're pregnant. Congratulations."

I took the ginger ale and shot her a smile. When Quinn made no move to reply, I said, "Pretzels would be great. Thanks."

She went behind the curtain and then popped back out. She lowered the tray table and set down a handful of packets before disappearing again.

"She's chatty," Quinn said, taking the cup from my offered hand.

"It's in her job description."

"Hmm." She took a sip and then leaned her head back against the seat.

"Was it bad the last time?" I asked softly.

"I don't really remember," she admitted "I was… consumed with other things."

With that one statement, it was a painful reminder that

I hadn't been there for her. That I'd left her needy, vulnerable, and grieving.

It was her turn to place her hand on my leg. "There are going to be a lot of moments where I say something or you say something, and all it does is remind us of our time apart. Of what we lost. I really"—she paused—"want to get to a point where it no longer feels like a knife to the stomach. Okay?"

We were the only two people on a commercial flight, and yet I still looked around, not wanting anyone to overhear our conversation.

"Give me your hand," I said quietly.

She immediately put her hand in mine.

"You can't say anything that would ever wound me more than what I've already done to us. So don't swallow your words, or your feelings. If you're angry, I want to know. If you're sad, I want to know. But please, don't keep me out of your bed. Or your heart."

She looked up at me and smiled.

"What? Too cheesy?"

Quinn laughed. It sounded light, easy, like the promise of our future wasn't hanging by a dark, frayed thread.

"No, not cheesy. Well, maybe a little, but it just made me think of when we first got together. How…dominant you were. Demanding. Wouldn't take no for an answer." She rested her cheek against my suit jacket. "You're softer now. Somehow. I like it."

"Never stop loving me, Quinn. I'm a work in progress."

"Aren't we all?"

Chapter 28

SASHA

The moment we landed in New York, Quinn's face became abnormally pale. I held her hand and asked, "Are you okay? Are you going to puke again?"

She shook her head.

"Then what is it?"

"We're in New York."

"*Da.*"

"Not Boston."

"I need to see Dimitri first. There's some business I need to take care of. Then we'll head to Boston."

She nodded, her gaze far away, seeing nothing. "Were you planning on us staying in your apartment while we're here?"

"Our apartment," I corrected. "And yes. It's still the most secure place I know of. It's a fortress."

"Do we have to stay there?"

I frowned and she rushed to add, "It's just that it doesn't—I don't have happy memories there."

My face ironed out. I grasped her hand. "We can stay

in the penthouse at The Rex. That's the second most impenetrable place in Manhattan. That okay?"

Her shoulders relaxed. "Yeah. That's okay."

I brought her hand to my lips and kissed the back of it. She shivered and closed her eyes, like she was sinking into it.

We got off the plane, and instead of going through customs, we went through the back door, trying to minimize our trail.

When we got into the car, she collapsed against the seat. "Is it weird that I feel like I'm being watched?"

"You are being watched," I said. "You've got to be aware. I don't know how he'll try to get to you, but he will." I just hoped he didn't take a play from the Igor Dolinsky playbook: drug her and carry her off.

Traffic was manageable, and it didn't take us long before the car pulled up in front of The Rex. A doorman opened the passenger side of the car to help Quinn out.

When she reached for him, I put a hand on her thigh to stop her. "Wait for me."

She looked like she wanted to argue but then thought better of it. I got out, looked around, surveying the area. I went to Quinn and took her hand and thanked the doorman who'd tried to help her. I got her inside as quickly as possible.

I strode to the front desk, Quinn still tucked in by my side. I gave the woman manning the counter a smile. She swallowed and her eyes widened. "We'd like to stay in the penthouse, please."

"I'm sorry sir, that room is already taken."

"No, it's not," I told her. "The penthouse is always empty unless Barrett and Flynn Campbell are in town. I'm a friend of theirs."

She pursed her lips. Apparently, she didn't know who I was. "Sir, I can't—"

Ignoring her, I pulled out my cell phone and dialed Barrett's number. She answered on the first ring. "Tell your staff who I am," I said.

"Hand over the phone," she said with dry amusement.

The woman took the phone from my hand and put it to her ear. "Yes? Oh, hello, Mrs.—I'm sorry I didn't—Yes, of course, right away." She handed the cell back to me, color staining her cheeks.

I put the phone to my ear. "Thank you."

"Yup."

She hung up and I slid the cell into my pocket.

The desk agent handed over two keys while stammering an apology. I flashed her a grin and said, "Don't worry about it."

Once Quinn and I were in the private elevator, she let out a laugh. "You enjoyed that."

"I kind of did."

"You get off on browbeating young women just trying to do their job?"

"Interesting choice of words," I murmured.

She shot me a questioning look. I backed her up against the polished wall and slid my leg between her thighs. Her eyes dilated with desire, and her lips parted.

My hands skated down to rest on the curves of her hips. She was tall yet slight. Sturdier than she looked. She'd withstood so much, carried so many burdens on her shoulders.

"I don't deserve you," I said in hushed reverence.

She cupped my cheeks with elegant fingers. Long, feminine. Everything about Quinn was beautiful, aesthetically pleasing.

Men had an insane need to possess the epitome of female beauty. They'd do anything for it. Launch warships, destroy countries. History was filled with countless stories about undeserving men riding off into the night for their women.

"Not here," she said.

The elevator doors opened directly into the penthouse. We stumbled out as we tore at each other, falling to the floor.

My lips met hers in a devastating kiss. I was taking everything she had and demanding more. Because I was a greedy bastard who wanted to stamp every inch of her skin with my lips, brand her as mine, beg her never to leave me.

But I couldn't take what Quinn wouldn't give. I didn't need to worry—because she gave everything. When my mouth grazed her flesh, I was owned. Bound to her. I was worshiping at the altar of Quinn, a humble servant on my knees, begging for a goddess to bestow her love on me.

"Sasha," she gasped when I slammed into her.

"I don't deserve you," I gritted, repeating my words as I pumped inside her body. "But I want you anyway."

Her arms wrapped around my shoulders, and she drew me closer, her body moving to meet mine. "I know," she whispered. "God, I know."

It had been so long since we'd been together, but I remembered the way to please her, remembered the way to move so that her eyes rolled back in her head. I didn't stop, not for a moment, not until she tightened around me, clenching, gripping me like she never wanted to let go.

"Quinn," I groaned, coming inside her with all the pent-up emotion I'd been carrying around for a year.

I was home.

Chapter 29
QUINN

"You have rug burns," Sasha said, drawing a finger down my back. "That would be my fault."

My head rested on my crossed arms, and I laughed. Truly laughed. It came from my heart, which felt light and free despite all that was hanging over us.

Sasha's hand moved lower to cup my bottom. "God, you're gorgeous. You know that, right? Do I tell you enough?"

"You do."

He was propped up on one elbow, peering down at me. Neither of us felt inclined to move to the bed just yet.

"I used to care, ya know? About how I looked. A lot. Because it had gotten me things. People treat you differently when you're pretty. When they think that's all you are."

"Poor little pretty girl," he teased.

I laughed. "No, I know how it sounds. Woe is me. My mother told me I was smart. So did my father But he let me model. God, as a teenager, it was all so confusing. I learned very early that it was easier to be pretty to get things than it was to work hard and apply myself."

I rolled over onto my back to stare at the ceiling. Sasha's hand rested on my belly, a solid assurance that he was there next to me.

"I can't believe I graduated college," I admitted. "That degree, every time I see that piece of paper, I cringe. My father bought it. Probably paid off some of my professors just to pass me. Michael O'Malley's daughter was not going to be a failure."

"You could've passed on your own merit. If you'd tried. I know that to be true. What does a college degree prove anyway? I don't have one."

My hand covered his. My fingers were cold, but the rest of me was warm. So warm.

"I was such a mess. A real party girl with a coke problem. But you know the difference between me and some other junkie?"

"What?"

"Money. And looks. Money opened so many doors for me. Looks let me walk through them. I was welcomed into clubs and bars before I was even eighteen. You think I'm so sheltered—and maybe I am."

I looked at him and stared into his ice blue eyes. "Dad kept me out of his business. I didn't even know Brandon was IRA until I was sixteen. Some kids grow up in it, weaned on it. Not me. I wish I had been. I don't think I'd be in this mess if I'd been involved."

He stared back at me—even the right eye, the blind eye. Half blind and he still saw more than anyone else.

"It's not too late," he said softly. "To leave this life behind." His gaze dropped to my belly. His touch was feather-light, like he was afraid to hurt the life I was growing inside of me.

"You'll never leave this life."

"I can't," he said quietly. "This is all I know."

"Those are my choices? Live with you or leave you."

"*Da.*"

"I've lived without you. I never want to do it again."

He drew me close and tucked me into the curve of his body. He threaded his legs through mine, so we were tangled together.

I pressed my nose to his chest, breathing him in.

"You don't have anything to prove," he said. His breath glided over my skin, causing me to shiver.

"What do you mean by that?"

He sighed. "I mean, I know how you held yourself against Barrett."

"There's no question if she's strong or beautiful or smart. She's all those things. She's a good mother, a good wife, and sometimes I just feel…"

"Like you can't ever measure up?"

"Yes. That. When we first met, I thought I—I thought I had to fight her for you, you know? Like no matter how much I loved you, it wasn't enough because she loved you more."

"Differently. She loves me differently. And now she loves you. She wouldn't have come to Italy to help me if she didn't."

"I know," I admitted, feeling guilty. Feeling *less* even though Barrett did nothing except be herself. "Sometimes I feel like she's so bright she's the focus, the one to revolve around. And it's not because I'm jealous of her. Envious, maybe? I don't know."

Sasha ran a hand down my back and brought me closer. "Before you, I was in love with her. Like, desperate, march-off-a-cliff-if-she-asked-me-to in love with her."

"You're not helping," I growled.

"Wait," he said, not laughing. "But I saw her with Campbell, and I watched how they were with one another. It's like they don't see anyone else. No one else exists for them. But I also saw their struggle. In the aftermath of Dolinsky. I realized that having her love as a friend was so much better. It was pure, unselfish, and it didn't come with all the fucking baggage. Their marriage survived because they both refused to let it do anything else. Two weaker people would've collapsed under the stress. Two *other* people in their situation wouldn't have made it."

"I don't begrudge her, Sasha. And I know it sounds like I…love her and hate her at the same time. But it's not that. I just… She's had a part of you that I'll never get."

"Ah, Quinn. She had a piece of me, sure. But it was a broken part of me. You"—he brushed his lips across mine —"put me back together."

Chapter 30
SASHA

We eventually moved to the bed and made love again. This time it was slower, less hurried but no less demanding. When Quinn slept, I slowly got up. I padded my way into the living room, closing the door of the bedroom so I didn't wake her.

And then I called Dimitri.

"You stateside?" he asked.

"New York," I confirmed. "We head to Boston tomorrow. Any word?"

"Found the agent who increased the restaurant policy."

"Yeah."

"He's dead."

I rubbed my forehead. "Well, isn't that interesting."

"Clearly he knew something and Marino didn't want him talking."

"What about the neighborhood?"

"Quiet. Not a whisper."

"Why the fuck would Ori Marino have his mother's restaurant set on fire to collect insurance money. What does he need that money for?"

"To pay someone off," came Quinn's voice.

I turned, phone still to my ear. She was standing in the doorway of the bedroom, wearing my undershirt. It hit her at the thighs, covering half the curve of her ass. She looked sexy and sleepy. And I wanted nothing more than to drag her to bed and keep her there. Keep her safe.

"I'll call you back," I said to Dimitri and hung up. I stalked toward her. When I was close to her, I cradled her cheeks in my hands and leaned down to give her a thorough kiss.

"Sasha," she said, tearing her mouth away and putting a hand to my naked chest. "Tell me what's going on?"

"I'd rather not."

Her mouth flattened. "If you tell me what you know, I'll tell you what I know."

"You know something?

"Maybe."

I sighed. "Marino had the insurance policy on his family restaurant increased and then someone set fire to it."

"Ori's family did it."

"Probably paid someone to do it. Not sure yet what he plans to do with the money."

She swallowed and her hand went to her throat; the diamond ring on her finger glinted in the low light. It bugged the living shit out of me that she wore another man's ring, but God forbid he found a way to get her back and realized she wasn't wearing it.

I peered at her. "What do you know?"

She bit her lip, clearly debating her words. Finally, she said, "When I was at the vineyard, I overheard Ori speaking to his grandfather. They were talking about revenge, and they mentioned the Drugovs."

The blood drained from my face. "Are you sure?"

She nodded. "I didn't think about it, until now, but that conversation came flooding back to me. Sasha? Who are the Drugovs?"

"Sit," I said, gesturing to the couch. "I need a drink."

"Not fair."

Her teasing tone didn't get the reaction out of me she wanted, and her smile fell. She went to the couch and sat down.

I headed to the bar and poured myself a glass of vodka. This was a home away from home. Barrett and Campbell stayed here whenever they were in New York. They used to have a place in the city, but when they made their permanent home in Dornoch, they'd sold it and chose to stay at The Rex when they came to town. It was comfortable and Barrett had redecorated in her style. It was as familiar to me as my own place. I'd spent many late nights here, discussing business, planning on how to combat our mutual enemies.

Shaking my head, I took a sip of vodka and then sat down in the chair perpendicular to the couch. "The Drugovs," I began, "were friends of Igor's father—Olaf." I looked at her and she nodded, so I went on, "Their daughter, Katarina"—her name was bitter on my tongue—"she murdered Igor's wife who was pregnant with his child."

Quinn's hand flew to her mouth, her eyes wide with horror.

"He came home to find her dead among the rose bushes she loved so much." My gaze looked to the window, staring off into the past.

"What happened to Katarina?" she asked, her voice a mere whisper, as if she didn't want to know the answer.

"We sold her. To a Mexican drug lord." I clenched the glass of vodka in my hand. "Guess her parents want retribution for that."

"But I don't understand," she said.

"Marino wants me to pay for Igor's death. And the Drugovs want their daughter vindicated. If Igor was alive, they'd want him dead. Since he's not—" I shrugged.

"So Ori and the Drugovs have a common enemy. You."

"*Da*."

She fell silent, her hands curled into fists in her lap.

"Ask," I commanded.

"Why didn't you ever tell me? About Igor's wife? About Katarina?"

"Didn't matter. It was in the past." There were things I never wanted Quinn to know. I'd never been a good man. But those later years with Igor… I'd done some things I didn't like thinking about. I'd made peace with Igor's death and how that all went down. After his wife died, he'd never been the same. The time after that, his reign had been filled with bloodshed and every ounce of humanity he'd had left was gone. I'd let him get away with things too. Things I should've battled for, but I'd been too much of a coward to tell him to stop. I hadn't wanted to challenge him. I hadn't wanted to lead.

"You can tell me," she said. "About your past."

"You want to hear how I was complicit in some of the most terrible acts a man can commit?"

She paled.

"I don't think you do, Quinn. Because right now, you think Ori Marino is a monster. But I've got news for you. I've done worse. To those that didn't deserve it. I've destroyed innocent lives. I've stood by and watched them become collateral damage. Why? Money. Power. Greed."

"I don't believe that," she said, her voice reed thin, wispy. "I think you did all that stuff for another reason."

"Do you?"

She nodded emphatically. "I do."

"Tell me then. Why did I do it even though I knew it was wrong and that I'd hate myself for it."

Quinn stared me straight in the eyes. Her gaze was green, glittering like emeralds. "Love, Sasha. Everything you've ever done has been for love."

Chapter 31
QUINN

I went back to bed alone.

Sasha needed time to himself. Time with a glass of vodka and the ghost that was never far from his thoughts.

It was strange, loving a man who wasn't good. He was a criminal. Violent, hard, powerful. But he'd never come at me with fists. He never tried to break me just because he could. And maybe I rationalized his past because I loved him.

Did it matter that he donated dirty money to charities? Did it matter that he killed in the name of love and loyalty?

He would kill for me.

He would kill Ori Marino for me.

Did I worry about his immortal soul?

Did I worry about my own?

I'd heard of men who murdered on a Saturday and went to confession on a Sunday. I understood the hypocrisy.

But I didn't claim to be religious. I was a lapsing Catholic.

My father greased the palms of the police chief and the mayor. Politics were dirty, just as dirty as the kind of life Sasha led.

My hand went to my belly.

My child would grow up in this world. I hadn't lied when I told Sasha I wasn't walking away. I couldn't. But how was I supposed to raise a child with a strong moral compass when his parents had enough money to make the needle point north? He would learn that money meant different rules.

Hadn't I known that?

As a teenager, I'd skipped school, and I'd never gotten into trouble. My father had bought my way out of it, every time. A new library. A new gymnasium. New athletic equipment for the football team.

Because that's what you did in families like mine. You used your money and influence to reshape the rules. Laws weren't for people like us.

Sasha's cell phone rang in the other room and he answered it with a low voice.

My fist went to his pillow, and I pressed my hand against it. How many years would we sleep next to one another? Would we even get that chance?

He claimed he was more terrifying than Ori Marino, but I wasn't sure. Sasha had never used my desire against me, never made my body betray me with the stroke of a finger or the flick of a tongue.

I'd lusted for Ori Marino.

And on our wedding day, he'd reminded me that lust wasn't logical. My body had reacted to his. More importantly, my heart had divided in two.

I'd left part of myself with him, a hopeful piece that wanted more than anything to believe he truly cared for me.

But I had to remember he'd used me, use me still, to get to Sasha.

I couldn't let that happen.

Sasha would never put me in danger, but I didn't see any other way. I'd been bait before—against my will.

What happened if this time, I was complicit? In on the plot from the beginning? Armed with knowledge and a brazen attitude?

Sasha had been right: if Ori had wanted to kill me, he would've done it already. What would he do if he knew I was carrying his child?

The door to the bedroom opened. "You're awake," he stated.

"Yeah."

"What are you thinking about?"

I rolled over and brushed the hair off my face. "Who was that on the phone?"

"Barrett."

"And?"

"Don Archer died."

"Who?"

"Don Archer—her contact at the FBI."

"Oh," I said, remembering the man. "He looked the other way when you and Flynn did your nefarious activities, and in exchange you turned over other criminals."

"*Da.*"

"Makes you a snitch, no?"

"I prefer to think about it differently. Campbell and I taking out competition."

"Call a spade a spade," I said, looking at the ceiling. "Snitch."

"What's wrong, Quinn?"

"I was just thinking about Ori."

He growled.

I sat up. "How is this supposed to play out? The two of you meet in a dark alley for an old-time duel? Shots at thirty paces? What?"

"I don't know."

"You don't know," I repeated. "He'll never let you get close to him."

"Probably not."

"And you won't let him close to you."

"Right."

"So? That leaves me."

"How do you figure?"

"I'm the Trojan Horse."

His blue eyes never wavered.

"Aren't I?"

He nodded once and then swallowed.

"Have you known all along?"

"Yes."

"Barrett? Flynn? Brandon? They knew too?"

He nodded again.

I cursed.

"Do you think I want to do this? Put you in this position? There's no other way, Quinn. Not that I can see."

"So you want to parade me around. A flower to attract the bee?"

"Not a bee. A fucking wasp. That guy stings to kill. You get me?"

"You don't think I know that?" I yelled, climbing out of bed. "Do you want me to kill him for you, too? Slice a dagger across his throat? Would that make this easier?"

He marched toward me so we were nearly nose-to-nose even though he was a few inches taller than me.

"Do you think I want my woman to have to kill her husband? Fuck no, Quinn. Do you think I wanted to ever put you in the position where you had to live with that on your conscience?"

I swallowed, not sure how to answer.

He took a step back, his face clearing of anger. "You still have feelings for him. That's what this is about. Not that you're bait. Not that we're dangling you like a carrot. You love him," he accused.

"Love," I spat. "Is one amino acid away from hate. And at the moment, I love and hate both of you. Do you think I like being a trophy to be fought over? Do you think I enjoy my position in this? I hate it more than you do."

"Doubtful."

I slapped him across the cheek. Because he was Sasha, he stood there and took it. Unflinching. Solid.

"I'm carrying his child. You think I can just reconcile that because I love you?"

I whirled, giving him my back.

A moment later, he closed the bedroom door. The room was quiet, and I was left listening to the sound of my beating heart.

Chapter 32
SASHA

The first hour in the drive to Boston was filled with tense silence. Quinn stared out the window and refused to look at me. She fiddled with the rings on her left finger, and it drove me insane.

I reached over to place my hand on hers, but she snatched it away, curling in on herself.

I wanted to demand she talk to me. Yell at me, scream at me, anything that gave me insight as to what she was thinking.

The divider between the driver and us was halfway down. I pressed a button to close it, so Quinn and I could have some privacy.

"Quinn," I began.

"Don't."

"Don't what?"

"Don't talk. I don't want to talk."

"Well, I do want to talk."

"I get confused after I talk to you."

"That's—"

She turned to face me. "I talk to you and think we're

talking to each other, but we're actually talking past each other. And every time I think I have it all figured out, you tell me…you keep…you're never honest with me."

"I know," I said with a sigh.

Her eyes widened. "I wasn't expecting you to actually admit it."

I rubbed the back of my neck, trying to find the words that would make her understand. "I know you don't want to be sheltered or protected, but it's…my job to protect you. And it kills me that I can't. Not really. Keeping things from you until I have to tell you, that's not protecting you. If I thought I could get away with it, I'd send you to be with your friends. I hate that you have to do this. That *we* have to do this."

"You don't have to do anything," she said. "It's all me. I married him. I'm pregnant. I'm the one suffering from the choices I made."

"It's *we*. Marino wants me dead. He expects me to be the one to come at him. He'd never expect you…"

"You're forgetting one very important fact."

"What's that?"

"I can't lie. My face shows everything."

"Then let it."

She frowned. "He's going to be on his guard—even with me."

"Absolutely."

"He won't let me out of his sight again. Don't you realize that if I go back to him, the only choice I have is to…" She swallowed, unable to say the words. "I don't know if I'm capable of it, Sasha."

My gaze hardened. "Him or me, Quinn."

"That's not fair. To put all of this on me."

"You can't have it both ways, *Myshka*. You can't be

upset when I don't include you and then balk when you have to do something difficult."

"This isn't something difficult," she said. "This is murder. Plain and simple."

I touched my right brow. "An eye for an eye?"

She paled. "It won't stop, though. We kill him and then what? Someone else steps up wanting revenge for his death."

"That's the life."

"The life sucks."

"I gave you an out. I told you to walk away."

Quinn's eyes drifted from mine to stare out the window. "How do I justify it to myself? If I do this…"

"You find a way. Or you let it eat you from the inside out."

Her hand moved to rest on her belly. I wasn't even sure she was aware of her action, but it told me plenty.

"Call Barrett," I suggested.

She snorted. "And ask her what? How she can so cavalierly dispatch violence?"

"She doesn't. She doesn't go looking for it, if that's what you mean. But she handles it. Because she knows no one else will protect her children the way she would. Instead of shying away from it, she learned how to shoot a firearm and fight and train. She refused to be a victim."

"Am I a victim?" she demanded.

"I think you like to play that card sometimes. Learn to defend yourself, Quinn."

"This isn't defending myself. We're talking about ending the man's life."

"Isn't it?" I pressed. "If you don't, you'll always be watching, waiting for him. You won't feel safe. You won't feel in control. These are the choices we make."

"These aren't a normal person's choices."

"You were never normal. Not in the family you grew up in, not when you decided to be with me, and not when you married Ori Marino."

She inhaled a deep breath but didn't reply.

"Look at me," I said, my tone soft.

Quinn reluctantly pulled her gaze away from the window and stared at me.

"I will not be punished for what you decide."

"What do you mean by that?" she asked with a frown.

"I mean, that if you decide you can go through with this, the plan, you will not punish me for feeling like I put you in this situation. Just like if you decide you can't do it, you won't punish me for killing the father of your child."

The color in her cheeks fled.

"Can you handle that, Quinn? Can you live with me after I do it?"

She didn't say anything for a long time, and I worried about her answer. But she put me at ease when she reached over and grabbed my hand.

"You won't have to do it," she said, tone firm with resolve. "I'll do it. You've done enough for me. It's time I took a stand."

I brushed the hair away from her cheek and then caressed her lips with mine.

"You'll live with me after I do it?" she asked.

I smiled. "Not only will I live with you after, I'll love you after, too."

Chapter 33
QUINN

We got to Boston and went to Shannon and Patrick's apartment. They weren't using it, clearly, since they were some place that Sasha refused to tell me. All he said was that they were safe.

Safe. Which meant I wasn't supposed to know. Maybe for their own safety. Maybe for mine, so Ori couldn't use the knowledge against me.

"It feels strange staying in their apartment," Sasha said, looking around the living room, still wearing his gray coat.

"We just stayed in Barrett and Flynn's place. That wasn't weird?"

"Different."

"Because you consider them family."

He shrugged.

"Shannon and Patrick are like family."

"Yours. They're your family. Barrett and Campbell are family to us both. It's different," he said again.

It was my turn to shrug. I wasn't going to argue with him.

EMMA SLATE

"Do you want to call and talk to Barrett?" he asked, finally taking off his coat.

"Why do you keep asking me that?" I wondered.

He peered at me. "So she can tell you what to expect."

I let out a strangled laugh. "She might've killed a man—"

"A few," he interrupted.

"A few," I corrected. "But she's never had to kill a man she called her husband."

"True. But she did have to kill a man she had unresolved feelings for. That's the same situation you're in, no?"

He didn't say it with any sort of accusation, just a general statement. An understanding.

"How can you be so blasé about it?" I demanded. "I thought it would drive you mad."

"It did. It does, but I know, at the end of all of this, I get you. I get a life with you, your love." His gaze dipped to my stomach and he smiled. "Our children. What does he get?"

I sighed and then nodded. "Yeah. Okay."

Sasha moved to sit down on the couch while I headed to the kitchen.

"I need food."

"You think they still have food in there? That's edible?"

"Ah, valid point. They always have something in the freezer, but it needs to defrost." I opened the freezer door. "Case in point. This lasagna."

"Italian food? Really?"

"That's irony for you." I set the lasagna on the counter and then opened the drawer full of take-out menus. I brought the stack to the couch and plopped down. As we looked through them, I couldn't stop the giggle.

"What?" he asked, looking at me in confusion.

The giggle became a full-on laugh. I laughed until tears

streamed down my cheeks. Sasha wrapped his arm around me and pulled me close.

"I know," he murmured against my hair.

"This is so weird," I hiccoughed. "We're sitting here discussing takeout, and tomorrow I'm supposed to…"

"Don't think about that now."

"I can't help it."

He rubbed my back, and his soothing touch calmed me. "Meeting with your lawyer tomorrow?"

I nodded.

"Any idea what he's going to say?"

"No. I hope like hell Ori hasn't fucked my father's company."

"I doubt that," Sasha said. "It's a lucrative enterprise. Set up perfectly for…"

"For?" I pressed.

He sighed. "For reallocating funds."

"Reallocating funds? You mean embezzlement?"

Sasha nodded. "You had no idea?"

"I mean, I guess I suspected." I groaned. "But no one wants to think of their father—"

"So don't. Remember him the way you want to. Leave it in the past; it has nothing to do with you."

"Except he gave me the company. I can't run it knowing what I know."

Sasha stroked his chin, looking thoughtful. His brow furrowed.

"What are you—"

"Hold on," he said. "I'm working something out."

I clamped my mouth shut.

Sasha shot up from the couch and started pacing. "He's taken control of your father's company, yes? That's what Donovan said?"

"Yes. Iron grip on it now. I doubt I'd get it back in the state I want it."

"So let him have it."

I stood up and marched toward him. "What did you just say?"

"Let him have it," he said again, still calm.

"Let him have a company that he stole? That was the only thing my father left me," I cried.

Sasha strode toward me. "Stop thinking like a sad teenager, Quinn. Your father gave you a hell of a lot more than a company. He gave you his brains and his pride. So start using them!"

I reared back like I'd been hit. "What's gotten into you?"

"I'm trying to get you to think like I think. Ori Marino will never give you back your father's company. He's running it now. He's been watching and waiting to make a move for years."

Rage poured through me. "That bastard thinks he can get away with it. I won't let him."

"You won't get it back, Quinn. You don't have the guns to go after him."

I bit my lip as I stewed and paced. "Guns. I don't have guns." I looked at him and smiled slowly.

He answered with a smile of his own. "What do you have, Quinn? What weapons do you have?"

"The kind he won't see coming."

Chapter 34
QUINN

The next morning, I walked through the revolving door of O'Malley Properties. I shot a smile at the security guard on duty and continued on my way.

"Miss? Excuse me!" he called after me.

He didn't know whom I was—he was probably new, someone Ori had hired.

Before the security guard could get to me, I was in the elevator with the doors closing. As I zoomed to the top of the building, my heart began a furious staccato.

I was a terrible liar, but I was an O'Malley, full of bravado. I'd spent my teenage years blowing through situations, refusing to back down, and flashing a flirtatious smile —and some leg—to get what I wanted. Why couldn't I use the same tricks on Ori?

The elevator doors opened, and I stepped out onto the floor. Nothing seemed out of the ordinary. People were working, typing away in their cubicles. A few gasps echoed through the room when they looked up and saw me.

I approached what used to be my father's office. Ori

had hired a young, blonde secretary who popped up from her chair like a jack-in-the-box.

"Hello, can I—"

I ignored her and went to the door, twisting the handle and stepping through the doorframe. Ori sat behind my father's desk, phone pressed to his ear.

He looked up when he saw me, his eyes widening ever so slightly. "I'll have to call you back," he said to the other person on the line and then promptly hung up.

I shut the door and stood there a moment, taking him all in. He'd removed his suit jacket and rolled up his sleeves. He looked exhausted but wired.

"Hi, honey," I said with a wide smile. "A blonde secretary? Really? Can you be more of a cliché?"

"Quinn. What are you doing here?"

I cocked my head to the side. "You don't seem happy to see me."

"Happy? I'm a little in shock." His face darkened. "You ran off with your boyfriend. On our wedding day."

"Funny thing, wedding days," I said, my tone mocking as I stalked toward him. "Most of the time, both parties are in charge of their faculties when they get married. It'll be interesting what the judge has to say."

"Judge?" He walked to the leather couch where he'd laid out his suit jacket. He quickly put it on and buttoned it. Ori's suit was his armor, and when he turned to face me, the man was fully composed. "Why are you getting a judge involved? Don't think we can work out our marital disputes on our own?"

I smiled. "Marital disputes. You're funny. You made a play for my company."

"You weren't really in a position to take charge." His gaze dropped down my body, no doubt taking in the black and white polka dotted dress and black pumps. "You look good, Quinn. Petrovich must be treating you well. Tell me, how long did it take for you to jump back into his bed?"

"Like it actually bothers you," I shot back. "We all know why you seduced me."

"Seduced *you*? Honey, you were begging for it."

"Oh, absolutely," I purred, sauntering toward him, like an animal on the prowl. "Neglected, grieving, bitter. You showed me how good it could be." I reached out and grasped his tie and dragged him forward—he let me, of course, because he was bigger.

His hands grasped my hips, and he hauled me closer, pressing his erection against me. "Why did you come here, Quinn?"

"Because you've been waiting for me," I said and swiped my tongue across my lips.

His eyes followed the movement, and he pulled me tighter against him.

"We have a lot of unresolved business between us," I said. "And I don't give a shit about what's between you and Sasha. That doesn't involve me. Not really. I know I'm just a pawn, but let's pretend for a second that you actually love me."

"I do love you." His head dipped.

I put my hand against his chest. "No lies between us, Ori. We've been through enough, and frankly, you know I'm a shitty liar. I can't hide anything from you. So please. If you can, give me the same courtesy. No more lies."

His jaw clenched. "Are you coming back to me? To be my wife? Or are you taking a stand—wanting to play whore to the Russian?"

My lips curled up into a wicked smile. 'Don't you know, love? I'm playing you both against each other."

He chuckled, but it was in sardonic humor. "I don't buy that for a second. You never stopped loving him."

"No," I admitted. "But ironically, I somehow fell in love with you too. So here I am. At a crossroads."

His fingers skated across my jaw, and to my consternation, lust unfurled in my belly, holding me captive between my thighs.

"Do you mean that, Quinn? Do you really love me?"

"Does it matter? In the end? What do you really want? Sasha dead because he took your best friend and your father's territory. I don't care about your vendettas. I don't want bloodshed, but getting you both to stand down is like asking two lions in the jungle to walk away from a fight."

"It was about that, originally," Ori said. His expression was still closed off, but I liked to believe I knew him, had the power to read him.

"It's not anymore?" I ventured to ask.

"I haven't slept well since I heard that my best friend had died. My father…he wasn't a good man. I know that. He was still my father. But Igor… We were brothers."

I bit my tongue from telling him Sasha felt the same way.

"You used me," I said. "And I know men like you. Men who live by their own strange code of honor. I want to appeal to that. Whatever you and Sasha feel like you have to do, I won't stand in the way. Hell, I'll let you two battle it out. I want nothing to do with it."

He brushed his mouth against mine and touched his tongue to my lips, demanding entrance. I opened for him —and I wished I could say it was a chore—but it wasn't. This was Ori. A man who'd said he'd never leave me. He hadn't. Through all of it, the push, the pull, the lies, he'd stayed. He'd remained true.

It had been Sasha who'd left.

I shoved against Ori's chest.

His mouth lifted from mine. "Quinn—"

I kept pushing until he was backed up against the desk. I reached for his belt buckle and then his zipper. My hand delved inside his pants, and I clasped him. His head reared back in pleasure.

Stepping forward, I lifted the hem of my dress and straddled his thigh. "This was never our problem, Ori." I ground against him. "Whatever lies bloomed between us, this wasn't one of them." I bit my lip as I pushed against him.

Call it survival, call it lust, call it the gray area. I'd do whatever I had to do to make it out of this alive.

Ori's hands clasped my hips as he brought our mouths together. His tongue parted my lips, and his hand slid between my legs.

"I'm not the villain," he commanded. "I'm your husband, and you are my wife. Fuck what any judge has to say. Your name is next to mine on a contract."

He plunged a finger into my wet heat, and I growled like a ferocious animal.

"You're a liar and a thief," I snarled, grasping the back of his neck and pulling him toward me, wanting to take him deeper.

All this time, I'd been trying to choose between two men when I should've been choosing me.

"Not a good enough thief," he rasped. "If I was better, you wouldn't love that bastard. The bastard who'd left you, the bastard who'd killed my best friend."

"And yet you came after me and everything I had to offer. You took my father's company. You took my legacy."

"One of my deepest regrets," he admitted, pumping me harder. "And yet I'd do it all over again. I'd do anything to win you."

"Honesty would've gone a long way."

"I never promised you honesty. I promised you this." His finger curled inside of me, and I saw stars.

I clutched his shoulders and held on while the orgasm ricocheted through me. I held him while I mourned the loss of our relationship, the loss of my naïveté.

"Come back to me, Quinn," he whispered, his teeth clasping my ear.

"I never left."

He withdrew his fingers and slid them into his mouth. "I'm hungry."

"Then take me to lunch."

Chapter 35
QUINN

I straightened my dress and then waited for Ori to right his appearance. Once he was finished, he held out his hand to me. I looked at it, feeling a pang of remorse.

Forcing a smile, I grasped it, and then we headed out of my father's office. The blonde secretary shot up from her seat, her brown eyes tracking Ori's movement every step of the way.

Jealousy, hot and fast, hit me in the chest I pressed myself against Ori's side. I stared her down, and she slowly sank back into her chair. "Your name?"

"Rachel."

"Rachel," I repeated. "Thank you for taking my husband's messages when we're at lunch."

"No problem," she murmured, her gaze following us as we walked to the elevator.

Ori's hand still clasped mine, and with the other, pushed the down button. "Still wearing your wedding rings, I see."

"And I see that you're not."

"Didn't think you cared."

"I do care. At least until we're divorced."

"We're not getting divorced."

I shot him a grin. "We'll see."

The elevator doors dinged open, and we stepped inside. Once the doors closed, Ori pressed me against the wall. "Now, where were we?"

"Down, boy," I said. "Stop mauling me in public."

"I thought that was my right. As your husband."

"You're my husband in name only. And only until a judge rules on it," I reminded him.

He smiled, like he found my threat empty and amusing.

It made me pause. It also made my nerves feel like trip wires. "Lunch first. Business after. Someone very wise taught me that."

His smile widened into a grin, and I was ashamed I liked seeing it. He grasped my hand as the doors opened, and we stepped out into the lobby. He took a moment to introduce me to the security guard, and then we headed outside.

"Is it me or has Boston been in the throes of winter for like a year?" I demanded. I hadn't worn a coat because I wanted to walk in looking sexy and powerful. I couldn't do that in a bulky winter coat that hid my body.

I shivered in the cold, and Ori brought me into the warmth of his side. I knew Sasha was somewhere close by, keeping tabs. I wondered what he thought when he saw me take comfort in the shelter of Ori's arm.

"Sure you want to go to a restaurant?" Ori asked, brushing his nose against my ear. "I could think of a more private place I'd like to take you."

"Food, Ori. Food and conversation. Sex clouds things."

The driver pulled to a stop at the curb. Ori opened the passenger side door, and I quickly climbed in, sighing when

I felt the heater blast my toes and fingers. He got in next to me. Ori told his driver where to take us and then wrapped his arm around me and brought his lips to mine

"I have to say I expected you to be far angrier than you are currently," I said, lips to his. I sank into his touch, telling myself it was for show.

"I let you run. You know that, right?" His fingers plowed into my hair as his mouth met mine again.

My hand went to the collar of his shirt, and I forced his tie to loosen. Then I was unbuttoning his shirt so I could see and feel the golden skin beneath.

"Did you fuck him?" Ori asked as I straddled him, the skirt of my dress riding up.

"Yes," I said without hesitation.

"Why?" he demanded, hands in my hair, holding my face steady.

"Because," I said looking him in the eyes. "I had to know what was still between us."

"And?"

"Nothing like what's between you and me." It was the truth but also a lie. Ori took it to mean more, as I intended.

"Why, Quinn?" he growled. His lips grazed my neck. "Why did you leave me?"

"Because I didn't trust you. I still don't trust you."

"And you trust him?"

"Fuck no," I said, letting true anger show. "He left me. How can I ever trust a man who did that?"

"But you went with him?"

"You lied to me," I pointed out. "Married me and lied to me while I didn't know who I was, who you were. Of course I left. And now you've taken over my father's company. You want to explain that?"

He smiled, a wickedly sexy grin. "Got you to come back to Boston, didn't it?"

"All a play," I said lightly. "I should've known."

"You don't seem that upset about it."

"We do this thing," I began.

"We? You and me?"

"Women," I said. "We're incredibly hopeful creatures. It's what makes us fall in love with a man's potential and not actually the man. To say I was angry at you"—I flashed him a smile—"was an understatement. You used me. Tricked me. Lied to me. But that wasn't what pissed me off the most."

"What pissed you off the most?" he asked, his voice soft, his expression genuinely curious.

"You made me love you," I said simply. "And I felt like an even greater fool for it. You embarrassed me." I let the anger I felt show in my eyes.

Ori's fury came back full throttle. "If anyone should be embarrassed it's me. You left me. *On our wedding day*. You remembered everything that day, went through with the marriage, and then left me. For your ex who walked out on you."

"Do not play the injured party!" I shouted.

"I'll play any damn card I feel like!" he shouted back. "And I took the helm of your father's company because you were too busy fucking another man to behave like the president of a multi-billion-dollar corporation. I had no idea where you were or if you were coming back."

I blinked. "So that gave you the right to—to step in?"

"Who else was going to do it, huh? Like it or not, we're married, we do share a last name, and I take my vows seriously. You obviously don't."

Chapter 36
QUINN

"You're delusional if you think those vows apply to us," I sneered.

"So it wouldn't bother you if you heard that I fucked my secretary on your father's desk?"

I slapped his cheek. It turned his head. A slight smirk appeared on his lips when he looked at me. "Thought so."

"You've admitted you wanted revenge on Sasha. You've admitted you wanted to destroy me because of my father's role in your family's demise. You told me you loved me, but you lied while I had amnesia." An errant thought crossed my mind. "Did you pay off the doctor? To tell me it was better if I remembered in my own time?"

His jaw clenched.

"You did," I said in understanding. "Why? For the sake of pure manipulation?"

"The night of the accident, you said you couldn't be with me because you didn't feel for me what you thought you should, and you were wrapped up in your damn feelings for the Russian. When I found out you had amnesia" —he swallowed—"I thought it was my chance. To make you fall in love with me. *Me*. And then if you got your memory back, I'd hoped you'd love me enough to give it a real try."

"Lies, manipulations… Why would you ever think that wouldn't weigh in my decision after I got my memory back?"

"Part of me hoped you never would," he admitted. He sighed and shook his head. "I've done a lot of terrible things. I've used you, I've hurt you. But everything I feel for you is real."

His tone was earnest and surprisingly sincere.

I hated it. It made me reevaluate things. My feelings, my plan, my life.

We pulled to a stop in front of a restaurant. I slid off Ori's lap and he climbed out first, and then he came around to help me. He took my hand and held me close as we walked up to the restaurant door. It was a charming little French café that was surprisingly empty. I looked at him in confusion.

"This is a café in the heart of downtown on a weekday and it's empty. Care to explain that to me?"

"I want to impress you. And perhaps seduce you with food. Into coming home."

I raised my eyebrows. "You really think we stand a chance? After everything that's happened between us?"

"You might change your mind after you taste the food. It might be the best in the city."

I clamped my mouth shut, refusing to give way to bitterness. But I didn't trust Ori—not with my food, not with my drink. He could have it drugged, and I would be none the wiser.

The hostess sat us in the corner and then discreetly left us alone. When the waiter approached, Ori asked for a bottle of Bordeaux and sparkling water.

Ashes

"Bold statement," I said, watching Ori remove his napkin from his plate and set it across his lap.

"What's a bold statement?"

"An Italian claiming a French restaurant is the best in the city."

The waiter returned with the water and wine. After he poured both, he left. No menus had been placed in front of us, so I knew the chef would send us food.

"You own this place," I said.

He smiled. "Guilty."

"All that time, claiming you wanted to open a new restaurant and head it yourself... Another one of your lies? Or was it not a grand enough life for you?"

"Grand? I don't want a grand life. My mother's restaurant taught me humble beginnings."

I snorted. "And your father's businesses taught you murder, destruction, mayhem?"

He grinned, and his eyes dipped to my mouth. "I've missed your tongue."

His double entendre had my cheeks flaming.

The waiter came with a platter of oysters and then he disappeared like a ghost. Whenever I dined with Ori, it seemed like the waitstaff was trained to be invisible.

"You didn't try the wine," Ori said.

I didn't hesitate and reached for the glass. The wine was complex, beautiful, and heady, like the man sitting across from me.

"Incredible," I said after swallowing.

"Try an oyster."

"Can't. Allergic," I lied.

"Mhmm. More for me." He picked up a jagged shell.

I couldn't endure a lunch that lasted three hours. I wanted to discuss business and leave everything on the table.

159

EMMA SLATE

He set the empty shell back on the platter of ice and looked at me. "I can have the next course brought out, so you don't have to wait until I finish."

"Thoughtful of you," I said, continuing the pleasant conversation dance.

Ori looked over my shoulder and nodded and a few moments later, the waiter brought two plates of steak tartare and set them in front of us.

I glanced down at the raw meat. My stomach churned.

"Allergic to raw steak too?" he taunted. "You're pregnant, aren't you?"

I gazed up at him and forced a smile, willing my heart rate to slow down. "Guess it's not really a surprise, is it? Since you planned it all along."

He stilled, his fingers pinching the wine glass. "When did you find out?"

"Few days ago. Saw a doctor. She told me I was further along than I thought. That's when I put the puzzle pieces together."

Ori dragged his tongue across his upper lip. "Petrovich…he knows?"

"Yes."

We stared at each other for a long moment. Ori took a sip of his wine and then cocked his head, looking thoughtful.

"I want a divorce," I said. "Not to be with Sasha—because we're not together. Carrying your child is sort of a deal breaker."

"Then why not stay married to me?" he wondered. "I love you. You know I do. We can be a family. Start over."

"There is no starting over. I want to raise the child away from this life. The danger, the violence. So please, I'm begging you. You say you love me. If you do, then let me go. Let us go."

160

"No," he said simply.

"You selfish bastard."

"I'm selfish because I want a life with the woman carrying my child? Explain that to me. And if you think I'm going to let you take my child away from me, you don't know who I am at all. So I've got a proposition for you, Quinn. Come back to me, and I won't take my child away from you when it's born."

"Fucking try," I said, my voice soft.

He smiled, a sinful, demonic smirk. "You think you can stop me?"

I leaned back in my chair and reached for my glass of wine. "Not about stopping you. But I don't believe you would be that callous—not to me."

"Oh really," he drawled. "How do you figure?"

"You should've killed me. It would've been easier."

"Probably. But what does that have to do with—"

"I know what you're doing with my father's company. You want to keep that going? I'll gladly sign away my shares to you. In exchange for a quiet divorce."

"I could kill you now."

"And your unborn child? No. You won't. Even you have a conscience. And maybe a little bit of hope? That this will all work out to your liking. Sasha dead, me by your side."

"You're playing a dangerous game, Quinn." His eyes glinted. "You sure you know the rules?"

It was my turn to smile. "I'm making them up as I go along."

"You asked me for truth between us. Are you sure you're giving me the same courtesy?"

"You want the truth. Here it is. I know you want to kill Sasha. I know nothing I say or do or promise will deter you from that path. But that's *your* path. It's a path that I don't want to go down. I want to take our child and live a different life. I want to go to brunch with friends and not worry someone is out to kill me or take my child and use him against me. I don't want *you* to use the child against me. Don't you see? It's all fucked."

"Did you want the baby? My baby?"

I thought about how to answer that was both truthful yet wouldn't give him hope. "I didn't know how to feel about it. At first. But I'd lost a child before and this felt like… another chance. When I think of the baby, I don't think of it as yours. I place no resentment on it for having you as its father. And I think, if circumstances had been different, we could be a family. But I can't, Ori. Not now. Not after everything."

He swallowed the rest of the wine in his glass and set it aside. The waiter tried to approach, but Ori waved him away. Clenching his jaw, he looked away from me and stared out the window.

"All right, Quinn. I'll grant you a divorce."

Chapter 37
QUINN

"I'll have my lawyer draw up the papers." I made a move to grab my purse, but Ori's hand on mine stopped me.

"Stay with me. Have lunch."

"Why?" I asked.

"Because"—his eyes found mine—"this is all incredibly sad. Don't you think?"

"Maybe a little," I agreed.

"You're pregnant with my child and you just asked me to give up all rights to it."

"Not in your plan?" When his eyes dimmed, I sighed, "Sorry. That was…unkind of me. I suppose I can stay and have lunch with you."

"What do you want?"

I raised an eyebrow. "Finally asking for my thoughts instead of just declaring an edict of what I'll eat?" I looked down at the steak tartare. "Will you please get this away from me before I vomit?"

Ori grinned and then gestured to the waiter who came over immediately and scooped up the offending raw meat.

"What would you like, Quinn?" Ori asked.

"Just a bowl of French onion soup, please."

The waiter disappeared again, and I shook my head. "I wonder how you trained them to do that."

"Do what?"

"Appear like they're not really here."

He winked. "Marino family secret." Ori's smile dulled. "Can I ask you a question?"

"Sure," I said, taking a sip of sparkling water.

"If I had done things differently. Not lied about our relationship in the hospital… would you have… Do you think this would've turned out differently?"

I took a roll from the breadbasket and tore a piece. "I don't know. You were…were really hard to walk away from that night."

"Then why did you?"

I searched for the words, wondering if now was the time to be honest, the time when it was all ending. "I was scared. You made me feel safe, and I was just waiting for the other shoe to drop."

"I'm sorry it didn't turn out how you wanted."

"I'm sorry it didn't turn out the way you wanted, too." Emotion clogged my throat. "Will you excuse me for a moment? Restroom."

He nodded and rose when I stood. I grabbed my purse and rushed to the ladies' room. Tears clouded my eyes, but it wasn't until I was in the privacy of a stall that I let them fall.

It was all so unbelievably sad. Were we all just a product of our circumstances? It would've been so much simpler if Ori never had feelings for me. Or if I'd never had feelings for him. And Sasha…

God, Sasha.

And now the baby, who I'd do anything for. Lie, steal,

cheat. Sell my soul if it meant being free of Ori Marino—no matter how conflicted I felt about him.

I heard the door to the bathroom open and then, "Quinn?"

"Please, go away," I sniffed.

"Will you come out?"

With a sigh, I turned the lock and opened the stall of the bathroom door. Ori looked as tortured as I felt. He held open his arms and after a moment, I went into them. He cradled me against his body and pressed his lips to my forehead.

"I'm sorry," he whispered. "I'm so fucking sorry."

I gripped his lapels, and my tears splattered his crisp white shirt. "Me too."

His fingers trailed underneath my hairline at the base of my neck. He wrapped his hand around my neck and applied pressure.

"What—"

I felt a thumb press into my skin, and then I felt nothing at all.

When I came to, I saw a white ceiling. My head was groggy, and my mouth tasted like felt. I thought I was in another hospital, but I didn't hear any beeps of machines. But when I tried to move my arms, they wouldn't budge.

Looking down, I expected to see an IV. Instead I saw straps cinching my wrists.

"You've got to be kidding me," I muttered. "Hello! Hello?"

The door to the room opened, and a doctor in a white lab coat entered. Sunlight glinted off his glasses, and he cocked a gray head at me.

His smile was calm—and condescending. "You're awake. That's good."

"Awake, yes," I said, trying to keep my tone placid. "Can you tell me where I am?"

"You are at Glenmoore."

Glenmoore was the psychiatric institution the wealthy and social elite sent their family members who needed monitoring.

"Why?" I asked, trying to still the panic.

"Your husband was afraid that you were a danger to yourself and your unborn child," he rambled. "So we're here to help you."

Oh, he was good, I'd give him that. Lying until the end. Refusing to accept defeat.

Instead of replying to the doctor, I leaned my head back against the pillow and shut my eyes.

"Just rest. You're safe now."

The door to the room opened and then closed.

Nothing to do but wait.

Chapter 38

SASHA

Three hours ago, Quinn had stalked into O'Malley Properties and then disappeared behind the frosted glass windows of the lobby. Twenty minutes later, she'd come out, Marino holding onto her.

Seeing his arm around her while he escorted her to the car had me ready to explode.

She was supposed to shoot me a text that everything was going according to plan. She was supposed to let me know that Marino believed her plea. But I hadn't heard from her.

While Quinn was occupying Marino, Dex and I had triggered the fire alarm. As the building evacuated, we snuck inside, bypassed the security cameras, and made it to Marino's office—the office that had once been Michael O'Malley's.

Dex was able to plug into the security system and automatically lock the building. No one was getting in. Then he blocked any calls going to Marino's phone.

"How long will this take?" I asked.

Dex logged on to Marino's private computer and began transferring data to his laptop.

"Few minutes. Dude, you need to chill."

"Sometimes, I'm amazed that you were able to hack into the FBI servers."

He grinned. "Took an afternoon. It was fun. Not nearly as fun as working for Barrett. Thanks for bringing me along on this adventure. I was getting bored."

A few minutes later, we snuck out of the building, and he erased our trail. We got into the car, and I took off at breakneck speed.

"Jesus." Dex grimaced as he reached for the door handle. "Slow down."

"No."

I got us back to Shannon's apartment, which we were using as a base. I unlocked the front door and stormed inside. I didn't bother removing my coat, knowing I'd be leaving in just a few minutes. "Time to find Quinn," I said.

Dex sat down on the couch and pulled out his laptop. He didn't look at all concerned, nor was speed his top priority.

"Where is she?" I demanded as I paced across the carpeted living room floor.

"Give me a second," Dex stated.

"You move too slow."

"Move too fast and you miss stuff. I'm sending all of Marino's data through a program I created."

"What will that do?" I wondered.

"It will ping suspicious activity and fake accounts. Since there's so much information to sift through, it weeds out all the noise and will just leave the little eggs he's trying to bury.

"And you made this program?"

"I did."

"Your talents are wasted."

Dex laughed. "I live for this stuff, you know? It gets me all—" He hunched over his screen and peered at it. He didn't look at all like a hacker. Dirty blond hair, athletic, very much a college frat boy. With a few taps of the keyboard, the screen changed to a map and a flashing red dot. He pointed to it. "She's right here."

"Is that coming from her phone?" I asked.

"No. From the skin tracker. Marino probably took her phone and threw it in some random garbage can."

My jaw clenched. At least I'd been one step ahead of him. Quinn hadn't wanted the tracker put under her skin —said it made her feel like a dog. She'd reluctantly agreed when she realized Marino never played by the rules, and she couldn't expect him to.

"She's at Glenmoore."

"Repeat that," I demanded.

"Glenmoore."

I cursed. "That fucker had her *committed*."

"No shit," he said, eyes widening. "You have to bust her out?"

"Looks like it," I said, tone grim.

"Why would he have her committed?"

"To keep her out of his hair. She must've deviated from the plan—or threatened him. He wants me occupied." I pulled out my cell phone and pressed Dimitri's number. I needed him and a few trusted soldiers to get here immediately.

Only when I called Dimitri's phone, another Russian answered.

The voice was cold and autocratic—one I hadn't heard in years but instantly recognized.

Aleksandr Drugov.

"Speak," Drugov barked. It wasn't directed toward me, but to someone else.

"Sasha?" came a weak voice.

Not Russian.

Not Dimitri.

Sean O'Malley. Quinn's brother.

"Sasha? Are you—"

Flesh smacked against flesh and then a moan.

"You can't win this war," Aleksandr spat. "I've been waiting years to make you pay for what you did to my daughter. Your girl is locked away, her brother is collateral, and your man…"

"Where's Dimitri?" My voice was low, harsh.

"Dead. You're done. Your territory is gone. There's nothing left for you."

"What do you want?" I demanded.

"You. In exchange for the brother."

"Like I buy that. You're colluding with Ori Marino."

Dex looked up from his computer. He frowned in confusion and pointed to his screen. I turned my back on him and focused on the conversation.

He rapped out a time and a place. "Come alone. You fuck with the plan and he dies."

Before I could reply, Drugov hung up.

Grief, anger, and impotence slashed through me. My second in command was dead. The brother of the woman I loved was being held and tortured. And Quinn…

Quinn was stuck in a mental facility. I couldn't save her. Couldn't protect her. Going to her would mean her brother would die.

"Hey," Dex said, waving a hand in my face. "What just happened?"

"So much shit I don't know where to begin," I said, my

tone grim. I shoved my emotions to the side. There was no time for them.

Chapter 39
SASHA

I had six hours to get everything in order. It wasn't enough time. And now with Dimitri gone... I swallowed. Too many of my brothers had died because of me.

Dimitri would be the last one. It would end with me.

"Who was that on the phone?" Dex wondered, his eyes searching mine.

"Aleksandr Drugov."

"Drugov," he repeated with a frown. "I know that name."

"He and Marino are in business together," I said for lack of a better explanation. It would take too long to go into all of it.

Dex shook his head. "No, that's not why I know him. He's on the list."

"What list?"

"The FBI's most wanted list. They've labeled him a terrorist."

My mind started to work again. It pushed through the grief and the fear, the guilt that everyone wouldn't be in this mess if it hadn't been for me.

This needed to end. It needed to end so Quinn could be safe and not have to look over her shoulder every moment. Marino and I were not just fighting over the loss of our best friend—we were now fighting for the woman we both loved.

"Don Archer died," I said suddenly. "Did you hear?"

His eyes dimmed. "I did hear. He was a good man and I—he's the only reason I didn't go to prison."

"Someone killed him," I stated.

"Yes."

"We don't have our connection at the FBI anymore. Archer—he was our back door. He took Barrett's tip-offs and in turn, he looked the other way when we needed him to. He was grooming someone to take his position, but he wasn't sure who he could trust."

"Jordan," Dex replied. "He trusted Jordan."

"Who is he?"

"She," he corrected. "Jordan's been on assignment in the field for a few months, so she hasn't been around. I wonder if she even knows Archer died."

"Why did he trust her?"

"Because she's his daughter."

"Archer has a daughter?"

"Don't look so surprised."

"I mean, it's just—he never talked about her."

"Did you talk about anything personal? I know Barrett has three children because I see them when I stay at her house. Archer was private, and he never wanted Jordan to be treated differently among her colleagues because of their relationship. She got promoted but deferred it to take one last case in the field."

"Do you have a contact number for her?" I asked. Tension buzzed under my skin. I was fighting the clock, and there were so many working parts I needed to take care of.

"Yeah, I have a direct line to her. But she may not get back to you in time."

"Well, she's our only hope."

"Why do you need her anyway?"

"Drugov is holding Quinn's brother hostage. In exchange for me."

"Shit." Dex's eyes widened.

I nodded once, my jaw clenched.

"He's going to kill you."

"I know that. There's not much I can do about it," I snapped. "If I can get ahold of Jordan, I can at least make sure that Sean has a chance of getting out alive. And she can bring Drugov in."

"Let me talk to her," Dex said. "You have a better chance of her trusting me than you."

"Why would she trust you?" I demanded.

His smile was slow.

"For fuck's sake. You were sleeping with Archer's daughter?"

Dex shrugged and pulled out his phone. "While I'm handling this, you handle what you need to handle."

I immediately created a bullet list in my head.

My first order of business was to call Brandon Kilmartin.

To my surprise, he answered on the first ring.

"I need your help," I said without preamble.

He paused and then said, "All right." His tone was serious and not at all teasing. Very unlike his usual self.

I quickly explained the situation.

"They have Sean?" he asked, voice filled with rage. "And Marino committed Quinn? What the ever-loving fuck?"

"I know."

"What do you need from me? Back up to get Sean out of there? I'm in Belfast, but I can be on a Concorde in thirty minutes."

"No. I'm supposed to meet Drugov alone or he'll kill Sean."

"You know you're going to meet Marino, right? Drugov won't just come out and say it."

"I know."

"You're walking into your death."

"I know that too," I said. There was no time for sadness, no time for mourning. There were those I loved whose lives meant more than mine.

He sighed.

"I need you to get Quinn out of Glenmoore. I'd expect an ambush, of course, but what the hell do I know? I haven't been able to guess any of Marino's steps."

"But you knew it was going to come to this, didn't you?" Kilmartin asked.

"Yes."

There had been a few moments after we'd gotten Quinn back and we'd made amends. We'd talked and made love, we'd planned for our future. I'd never been one for delusions, but a part of me really hoped I would've been able to end this. Maybe I could have, if the Drugovs hadn't been involved. But it was too much, and I was drowning. Every time my head came above water, another wave crashed over me.

"Get her out of there and take her somewhere safe."

"I'll take her home with me. Is that all right?"

"Yes." I paused. "Don't tell her what I plan to do. Don't tell her about Sean."

"I won't."

"Thank you." We were just about to hang up when I said, "One more thing. She's pregnant, Brandon."

Chapter 40
QUINN

Sunlight streamed through the clear glass window. I saw the branches of a tree, devoid of leaves. I wondered how it would look in spring.

I wondered if I would still be here in spring.

My arms were still strapped down to my sides. I was unable to move. Ineffectual.

Time and time again, Ori Marino proved to me I was a fool. A powerless little princess trying to play the part of a queen. Time and time again, Ori Marino outsmarted me, outmaneuvered me, outthought me.

Sasha hadn't come for me. He always came for me—even when he was late. Which meant the plan had been blown to shit.

I was on my own. Trapped in a psychiatric ward where I didn't belong.

The door to my room opened, and an orderly walked in with a tray of food. "Time for an afternoon snack," he boomed and shut the door with one hand.

He turned around and winked.

Brandon Kilmartin was here.

"What happened to him? He was supposed to come," I whispered.

"I'll explain later," he said and pulled up a chair to sit down. "Right now it's about getting you out of here."

"How do you expect to do that? There are security measures—"

"Hey," he said with a charming grin. "I've got this. Trust me."

I nodded.

"They give you any meds?"

I shook my head.

"Good."

He picked up the spoon and fed me a bite of a pear drenched in syrup. It was sickeningly sweet, and I turned my head away and closed my eyes.

"Nauseated?" he asked.

I opened one eye and peered at him.

"I know," he said, his tone soft.

"No one was supposed to know."

"He told me."

"Why? So you can be gentle with me? Coddle me?"

"Lock it up, Quinn," he commanded. "Now is not the time to lose your shit." He set the tray on the small table in the corner and then came back to sit in the chair by my bedside. He leaned over me.

"What are you doing?" I demanded.

"If anyone walks by, they'll see an orderly checking to make sure you're secure. But really, I'm undoing your restraints. The timer on my watch will go off in"—he glanced at his wrist—"two minutes and ten seconds. And then we're getting out of here."

I didn't ask how, because this was Brandon. He paid people, he planned, he had a way. If he said we were getting out of here, then I believed him.

His watch timer went off, and he silenced it immediately. Brandon went to the door and then waved me to him. "If we see anyone, you keep quiet and your head down. Let me handle it." He grabbed the container of syrupy pears and dumped them over my head.

"What the fuck!" I hissed as the sugary liquid ran down my neck.

He grinned. "Gotta have a reason to get you out of the room. You need to be hosed off."

I growled at him.

With one hand, he opened the door. With the other, he grasped my arm. I stumbled and righted myself. Everything looked white and unfamiliar. When I'd awakened here, I'd already been in a room, strapped down.

We turned down a corridor. Two men were approaching us. I tensed, but Brandon didn't appear at all concerned. One of the men was dressed in all white like Brandon. The other wore a white lab coat—probably a doctor.

They nodded at each other, and then we continued on.

I breathed a sigh of relief as we kept walking.

"Hey!" a voice called.

My shoulders tensed, and then Brandon spun me around, his hands gripping my arms, hard enough to leave bruises.

"Hey," Brandon called.

Another orderly jogged toward us. "What are you doing with her?"

"She needs a shower," Brandon drawled. "The crazy bitch decided to douse herself in pears."

The orderly's brown eyes narrowed. "Why was she out of her restraints?"

"Said she could feed herself." Brandon's shrug was negligent, uncaring.

"Who's your superior, I don't recognize you."

Brandon held out one hand—the hand not holding me. "I'm new. Jonas Wilkinson."

My lips twitched at Brandon's alias. Jonas Wilkinson had been a friend of his when we were teenagers.

"Your superior?" the orderly snapped, not taking his hand.

Brandon sighed. "Damn it." He shoved me away from him and lunged for the orderly. The guy didn't get far. Brandon slugged him across the jaw, hard enough to knock him out.

"There's a closet over there," Brandon said, picking him up. "Open the door for me, will you?"

I rushed to the door. Brandon shoved the guy into the janitor's closet and jammed the lock.

He grasped my hand, and we took off at a jog.

"Punching him was the only option?" I asked in amusement, adrenaline finally making its way through my blood, shaking off the malaise.

"No. But it was certainly the fastest."

The syrup was now dry and caked to my skin. My hair was crunchy, and my annoyance at Brandon Kilmartin for the pears over my head knew no bounds. All of that went out the window, when Brandon opened a door, and fresh air and sunlight greeted me.

We jogged across the pavement, my bare feet prickling with cold.

"Sorry," Brandon said. "I couldn't bring anything in with me, otherwise I would've grabbed you some boots or something."

"It's okay," I wheezed.

We were in a parking lot, which was full of staff cars. I looked behind me, expecting to see a swarm of men in white coming for me. But the door to the facility remained closed.

"How did you do it?" I asked.

"A well-timed diversion."

"Meaning?"

"I set off a bunch of M-80s in the basement. They're loud but don't do any damage and people will go investigate. Ah, here we are." He stopped in front of a blue Buick which was idling. He opened the back door, and I jumped inside, desperate to get warm.

I was wearing a hospital gown and nothing else. There was no dignity in a hospital gown.

"We ready?" the driver asked.

I recognized the voice immediately and grinned. "Hi, Colleen."

Brandon's younger sister met my eyes in the rearview mirror. "Hey, Quinn. You got yourself in it, haven't you?"

Chapter 41

QUINN

"You brought your sister?" I asked in amusement.

"You're supposed to say thank you," Colleen said dryly.

"You brought an Irish girl to drive on American roads as backup? Colleen, we drive on the opposite side of the road, just so you know."

She flipped me the bird. "Clothes are in the bag down below for you."

"Ah, bless you guys."

"Crouch down," Brandon said. "Just in case. I'll tell you when it's safe to sit up."

"You married a real bastard," Colleen said.

"No kidding. So are you going to tell me why Sasha couldn't come for me himself?"

Colleen and Brandon exchanged a look.

"No," I snapped. "Do not do the Kilmartin sibling thing where you speak without words, and no one has any idea what you're not saying. You did it when we were kids, and it bugged me then too."

I saw Brandon wipe a hand down his face.

"You're not supposed to tell her," Colleen said.

"I'm strong enough," I said. "Tell me."

"Have you heard of the Drugovs?"

"Yes. Sasha told me who they are."

"They're working with Marino. And…they have Sean."

I blinked. "My brother? How?"

"Don't know," Brandon admitted. "But the Drugovs are holding him hostage."

"What do they want? Money? I've got money." My mind went into a frantic whirl.

"Quinn." Brandon's voice was gentle.

"No," I gasped. "No, they can't. He won't—"

"It's done. Sasha is meeting them in a few hours. Aleksandr Drugov will release Sean once Sasha turns himself over."

"Bullshit," I snapped. "They won't let Sean live. Sean could identify them—"

"This is the end, lass," Brandon said gently. "There's no way to play this. We don't have any trump cards. *Deus ex machina* doesn't exist in real life."

I felt hollow.

Sasha was sacrificing himself for my family. For me. Ori couldn't win. I wouldn't let him win.

"He asked me to get you somewhere safe," he said. "So we're going to Belfast."

"Not yet," I said, firm resolve coating my voice. I straightened my back.

"What are you thinking, Quinn?" Colleen asked.

"I won't take you to New York," Brandon stated.

"You know where the meeting is?"

"No," Brandon said too quickly.

"Eejit," Colleen muttered.

"Why do all the women in my life call me an eejit?" he demanded. "You, Barrett—"

"Because you're an eejit who can't keep his mouth shut," I snapped.

"No? You don't want to storm the castle and try to negotiate with Marino?"

"No. Because that's exactly what he expects me to do," I realized aloud. "He thinks he can manipulate me by using Sasha."

"Can't he?" Colleen wondered.

"Once upon a time, maybe."

"But he'll kill Sasha," Brandon stated. "We can't let him."

"You know the time and meeting place, don't you?" I said.

"Yes."

"Because Sasha told you."

"Yes," he said in exasperation. "I don't follow you."

"You don't have to. Colleen, turn right up here."

Colleen put on her turn signal and followed my direction. "Where are we going?"

I grinned, finally thinking like Sasha. "I'm going to see a powerful friend."

"Who?" Brandon demanded.

"The Mayor."

Colleen and Brandon exchanged another look.

Brandon swiveled around to glance at me. "What are you going to tell him?"

"Don't worry about it."

"Quinn," he growled.

"Brandon," I growled back.

Colleen pulled to a stop. "Are you sure you want to see him looking like you do?"

"I'll clean up in the bathroom."

"How do you even know he's in his office?" Brandon asked in exasperation.

"Because I do."

"How do you know he'll see you?"

"If he wants to get re-elected, he'll see me."

"I like this new Quinn," Colleen said with a grin.

I flashed her a smile and got out of the car and quickly dashed inside the building. I checked in with the security agent, told him my name, and that I didn't have an appointment.

"The Mayor doesn't take meetings unless it's on his schedule," the man said.

"I know. Tell him who I am. Tell him it's urgent."

With a roll of his eyes, he reluctantly picked up the desk phone and made a call. "Hi, Jeanie. It's Bob. I've got Quinn O'Malley down in the lobby. Says she needs to see the Mayor and it's urgent. Sure, I'll wait." He looked back at me. "She's just checking with him now."

His tone was condescending, but I took extreme pleasure in watching his face fall. "Okay, I'll send her up. Thanks, Jeanie." He set the phone back down. "Uh, you can go up now."

"Thanks, Bob. I'll just hit the ladies' room real fast."

I sauntered to the restroom and ducked inside. Looking in the mirror, I grimaced. I took a paper towel and got it wet. I scrubbed my neck and then did the most I could with my hair. It was damp and flat against my scalp—and I really wished I'd had time for a shower and a change of nice clothes, but desperate times, here.

I left the bathroom and then headed up to the Mayor's office. The secretary glanced up from her desk and smiled. "Hi, are you Quinn?"

"I am."

"Great. The Mayor is on a call. He'll be done in a moment. Can I get you something to drink while you wait?"

"Water would be perfect, thanks."

She got up and went down the hall. A moment later, she returned with a glass of ice water. I sipped on it while I paced around the waiting room.

Finally, the office door opened and the Mayor stepped out. "Quinn," he greeted with a wide smile. He wrapped me in a hug and then opened his arm to show me to his office.

"I haven't seen you since the night of the gala."

"Whew, yeah, the gala," I said with a taut laugh. When my entire life had changed only I hadn't known it yet. "I'm sorry to show up unannounced without an appointment. I don't have a lot of time, but I need your help."

He sat down in the chair and crossed his hands on his desk. "What can I do for you?"

I took a deep breath. "I need you to denounce O'Malley Properties. Publicly."

Chapter 42
QUINN

Mayor Brigsby was a good poker player. I knew that because my dad used to play cards with him and the police chief once a week. Dad always cursed that the Mayor gave away nothing and that's how he was able to take the pot of three thousand dollars with a pair of sixes.

"I'm not sure I understand," the Mayor said slowly.

"I think you do," I said. "Look, I know my father funded your campaign and put you in office. And I know you know where my father got his money."

He stiffened. "Are you threatening me?"

"Not at all," I said with the shake of my head. "You know my father left me O'Malley Properties, don't you?"

"Yes."

"Well, that company is no longer in my control."

"What do you mean?"

I held up my hand and showed him my wedding ring. "I married a very terrible man, Mayor."

"Donovan called me, but he didn't give me a lot of details. Just said that you were out of the country and someone else was running O'Malley Properties in your stead."

"My husband is now in control of my father's company. He's laundering money, funding illegal causes."

"Who did you marry, Quinn?"

"Ori Marino."

"Nice Irish girl like you married an Italian?"

A smirk appeared on my lips. "That's the least of my worries."

The Mayor sobered. "If I do this, that's the end of your father's reputation in Boston. It'll be blown wide open: the corruption. There will be an investigation, assets will be frozen, your privacy will be non-existent. The papers are going to get ahold of this and trash the hell out of you. You sure you want to do this?"

"Only way to stop him," I said. "I asked for a divorce, and he wouldn't grant me one. So I'm taking it to the next level."

"You mean by having him thrown in jail? You could go down too, Quinn. For doing the same thing. You did take over your father's company."

"Pretty little Quinn who wasn't smart enough to run her father's company, so she asked her husband to step up and do it?"

He leaned back in his chair. "You really want to play that angle? We can."

Did I want to portray to the world that I was stupid and needed a man to run things? No. Of course not. But at the end of the day, I wanted Ori Marino to fall. He'd know I was the one to bring him down. That was enough for me.

"I'd like to play that angle," I said quietly. I cleared my throat. "He'll try to leave the country, but I know where he's going to be in"—I looked at the grandfather clock behind the mayor's head—"two hours."

"Please tell me he'll be in Boston."

I shook my head. "New York."

He sighed and reached for his phone. "It's going to take a god damn magician to pull all this off in time."

"That's why I came to you," I said with a bat of my eyelashes.

The Mayor chuckled. "I get why men never say no to you."

"Believe me, I'd prefer it if they left me the hell alone."

"Give me a few minutes. I'll make some calls."

I got up from my seat and exited his office, closing the door behind me. I was sick to my stomach. Could've been the morning sickness, but more than likely, it was my fear for Sasha. I did worry about my brother—another O'Malley used as bait to draw out Sasha Petrovich.

Sasha would sacrifice himself for my brother in a heartbeat, because he wouldn't want me to suffer through another loss. It was selfless, the kind of action that made epic stories epic.

And it was fucking stupid.

But Sasha would never put me in a position to choose between him and my brother, so once again, he'd taken the choice away from me.

I took a seat on the couch and waited. The Mayor's secretary was gone, so it was just me in the quiet office.

Brandon's words cycled through my brain. He'd given up hope, clearly, that there was no way to stop Ori from killing Sasha. But I had to try. What would stop Ori? Could he be stopped?

My hand went to my belly as my brow furrowed in thought.

The door to the office opened, and the mayor stepped out, buttoning his suit jacket. I jumped up from my seat.

"Made some calls. Got the warrant in the works. Had to let the Mayor of New York know what was going on in his jurisdiction."

"I need to get to New York, and I need to get there fast."

He nodded. "We'll take the helicopter."

Chapter 43
QUINN

Brandon and Colleen were quiet as they sat in the helicopter, staring out the windows as we descended into Manhattan. They'd grown up with everything they ever needed, but their parents were modest. No show of wealth. Not at all like me.

Riding in a helicopter was nothing to me. My senior prom date had taken me to the dance in his father's helicopter. He thought it would've helped him get lucky. It might've—if he hadn't gotten drunk and then puked on his tux.

That was sort of a mood killer.

The helicopter landed, and I unbuckled my belt. When we were clear to open the doors, I burst out and nearly fell to the ground.

"Quinn!" I heard Brandon yell.

I stopped even though I wanted to keep running, but I didn't have a phone or a wallet, or anything to get me where I needed. So I waited and turned. Colleen and Brandon were jogging up behind me.

Colleen shoved a coat at me. "You forgot this."

I was running hot, so I didn't feel the cold air or the bite of the wind. I relished it.

"I need you both to do something for me!" I yelled over the noise of the propeller.

"What is it?" Brandon asked, clearly pissed at me for being here when I told him I had no plans to go to New York.

"Don't try to stop me from what I want to do."

They gave each other the Kilmartin look, and then Brandon sighed. "I'm not going to like this, am I?"

"No. You're not." I looked at Colleen. "I need to make my own choices."

She held my gaze and then nodded. "All right, Quinn, I'm with you. Brother?" She looked at Brandon who reluctantly nodded.

"I'm with you, too."

I glanced over his shoulder to the Mayor who was striding toward us. I moved past Brandon and Colleen and went to him. "I have to go. You've got things working on your end?"

"I do. I won't give them the signal until it's time."

"You have Brandon's number. He'll be with me if you have to get ahold of me."

He put a hand to my shoulder. "Be careful."

His gray eyes stared into mine. I put my hand over his and squeezed. That was the thing about love. Nothing careful about it.

"I will," I lied.

Brandon, Colleen, and I got down to the street. I pulled on my jacket just so I wouldn't have to carry it. There wasn't a lot of time to get downtown, find what I needed, and then head to the meeting place.

"Should we catch a cab?" Colleen asked.

"Subway," I stated. "Faster."

Brandon made a face. "Subway? Really?"

"This is my operation, Brandon."

He rolled his eyes, and then we took off for the nearest subway station. We dodged tourists and surly Manhattanites. Because it was rush hour, the platform was packed. A train came almost immediately, and we shoved on.

"This must be what a cow feels like," Colleen remarked from somewhere near my armpit. We were packed together, and it smelled like body odor and corned beef.

Nausea instantly rolled inside my stomach. I burrowed my face into my coat collar and closed my eyes, willing the nausea to pass. I focused on my breathing until Brandon nudged me. I looked up and saw our stop. We pushed out of the train car and onto the platform. When we got above ground, I breathed in a few gulps of fresh air. Well, fresh for New York, anyway.

I quickly got my bearings, noting all the Chinese signs. Brandon and Colleen were talking, but I hardly noticed. I closed my eyes, trying to remember the name of the Chinese restaurant that would have what I was looking for.

I started to walk, not caring if Colleen and Brandon followed. But I knew they were behind me even as their words fell silent. It was nearly dark, and the lights of Manhattan bloomed into brightness. People were eager to get home, out of the cold, but I felt invigorated, filled with purpose.

The streets all looked the same, and I turned down many wrong ones and had to backtrack. Frustration dogged my heels, along with the knowledge that time was ticking away.

"What are we looking for?" Colleen asked.

"A Chinese butcher? That one has chickens in the window."

I didn't smile at Brandon's attempt at levity. I stopped walking because I saw the sign. "Here. I'm here."

I looked up at the neon yellow sign with writing I didn't understand.

"You sure?" Colleen asked. "They all look the same."

"I'm sure."

The three of us stepped into the restaurant. The smell of fried wantons and duck hit me. I inhaled greedily. If I'd had more time, I would've considered eating.

We walked up to the hostess, an older woman with dark hair in a bun streaked with gray. Her brown eyes looked to each of us. She held up three fingers and gathered the menus.

"I'm looking for Lin," I said quietly.

She slowly set the menus down. The woman stared at me and then eventually nodded. She waved me to follow her.

"You guys stay here," I said to Brandon.

"But—" he protested.

"My rules."

"Fine," he mumbled. "Think I can get an egg roll to go?"

"If you can make it fast," I stated and then turned to follow the woman.

She led me through the busy restaurant, toward the back. We went through the kitchen, and she stood in front of a gray metal door. She rapped three times. A moment later, she opened it and then urged me on.

With a deep breath, I entered the darkness. I took the stairs slowly, holding on to the wall. There were no lights to show the way. When I got down to the last step, I looked into the room. It was large and sparse. A long table and chairs. A mini fridge. I wasn't sure what to expect of a place like this.

A man in a dark suit stood by the table. Handsome and lean. He peered at me as I strolled closer.

"I'm friends with Barrett Campbell."

"What can I do for you?"

"I need your help," I said.

His eyes darkened. "Have a seat."

Chapter 44
SASHA

I walked into the warehouse and was instantly transported back in time—to another warehouse—to protect a different woman.

The smells were different. This warehouse was musty, moldy. Empty. Devoid of use. The cement floor was stained with oil and paint, and the fluorescent lighting buzzed and flickered.

There was no one in the room, not even Quinn's brother. My heart tripped in fear that Sean was already dead, and this would have been all for nothing. But Aleksandr Drugov was not a man to bluff—and neither was Ori Marino.

I heard the sounds of footsteps, and I turned slowly. I didn't expect to be shot in the back. No. Both these men wanted to see the life leave my eyes. They'd face me when they ended me.

Ori Marino stepped into the warehouse and stopped. He surveyed me, dragging his eyes over my scarred face.

"Jesus, you really are ugly, aren't you?"

I smiled, projecting lazy insolence. "Quinn doesn't seem to mind."

"Quinn didn't seem to mind my looks, either."

Clenching my hands into fists, I kept them firmly by my sides.

"Don't like hearing that, do you?" he sneered. "You probably wouldn't like to hear that I made her scream my name."

He was trying to rile me, but I refused to let him. "Let's not do this. You got me here. I'm unarmed." I lifted my pant legs to show him I wasn't stashing weapons. Then I opened my suit jacket to do the same.

"We both know that you don't need a weapon to kill me," Marino said lightly. "And we both know you won't kill me."

He was right. I wouldn't try to kill him. Not until I could ensure the safety of Quinn's brother. "Sean?"

"With Drugov."

"Not here?"

"No."

"Why not? I thought he'd want a piece of my hide."

Marino looked thoughtful. "He and I have our own deal. He knows this—between us—is personal. He's just happy to know you're going to die."

"But Sean?"

"Roughed up a bit. But he'll live. Can't have my own brother-in-law murdered." He grinned. "Can't anger my wife, can I?"

"I think you angered her plenty when you had her committed."

"Of course that's the conclusion you'd jump to. I wanted her protected. I wanted her safe. I knew I couldn't do it. Not while I tended to this."

"She's not yours to protect," I snapped.

"But she is. She's the mother of my child. She's my wife." He snorted. "Can't believe she asked for a divorce."

"You love her."

Marino's dark eyes glittered. "I do."

"Funny way of showing it."

"I could say the same about you. What kind of man walks away from the woman he loves? I never walked away."

"You didn't live through what I lived through. You have no right to make any sort of judgments about it."

Marino's gaze hardened. "When Quinn cried in my arms over *you,* then I have plenty of judgments to make."

"You used her and manipulated her—and then you got her pregnant."

He grinned. "I win."

"It's fucked, you know," I said softly. "We've loved and lost the same people and yet we both handled it so differently."

"Are you haunted by the things you've done?" he asked, his smile slipping.

"Are you?"

He chuckled, but it was bitter, hollow. "God, doesn't this feel like a conversation to be having in a dark library over drinks? And not here, in this warehouse?"

"Can we get on with this?" I demanded. "My life for Sean's. Swear to me. On your love for Quinn. On your love for your child."

He held my gaze. "I swear it."

"Your word is complete and utter shit, Ori Marino," Quinn said mildly as she strolled into the warehouse.

I turned. "What are you doing here?"

She kept her gaze on her husband. "Saving your life, of course. What do you want, Ori?"

"I thought I made that clear," he drawled, not seeming surprised to see her.

"You want Sasha dead."

Marino nodded.

"Is there anything that can be bartered for his life?" she pressed. "My life for his."

"I don't want *you* dead," Marino said. "I want you alive. I want our child alive."

"But with you. As a family?"

"You just asked me for a divorce."

"I take it back."

"You what?" I demanded.

Quinn didn't even look at me. She was completely focused on Marino.

"I'm not sure I understand," Marino said slowly.

"You, me, the baby. We'll be a family. I'll build a life with you. I'll stand by your side. If you let this go. Let the anger and the vendetta go."

"I can't," Marino said. "You're asking me to give up everything I've been working for. Years in the making."

"Love or hate." Quinn said with a nod, and then she finally looked at me. "And I choose love."

I frowned. "What are you—?"

She pulled something out of her pocket, a little white tablet the size of a nickel. "Know what this is?"

"I couldn't claim to, no," Marino replied.

She looked at it one final time and then popped it in her mouth. A few moments later, she opened her lips. "Gone. See?"

"Quinn," I whispered. "What did you do?"

"It's a concentrated lethal dose of Chinese herbs. I'll be dead within minutes." Quinn smiled and reached out to touch my cheek.

"I'm the linchpin in all this. Remove me and it all

crumbles." She pressed her lips to mine. "I love you," she whispered and then collapsed to the ground.

Something inside of me shook and vibrated. Every loss, every moment of grief, everything I didn't have time to mourn, came at me with a force. I channeled hot blistering rage into calm, lethal dedication.

I forced my gaze away from Quinn's still form to look at Ori Marino. He'd dropped to his knees. His face was a broken mask, his eyes glazed with disbelief.

I used his distraction to tackle him to the ground. My fists found his jaw. I pummeled and beat the living shit out of him.

He didn't fight back. Didn't even raise a hand in defense. With each punch, he shrank. Smaller and smaller until his eyes were nearly swollen shut, his nose broken and bleeding. I didn't even feel my knuckles bruise.

I heard a howl—and realized it was coming from me. It was the same noise I'd made when my father used me as his ashtray. It was the same noise I'd made when I watched my brother drown.

Wails and the sound of pounding flesh.

"Enough," someone said.

It took three people to pull me off Ori Marino's body.

I just needed one more minute to bash his skull in.

"Enough, brother," Brandon Kilmartin said. His eyes were somber as he took in the scene.

Before I knew it, I collapsed against his shoulder and bayed like a man who'd lost the love of his life.

Chapter 45
SASHA

The swarm of commotion didn't penetrate my numb senses. It was like I was underwater, deaf, mute, drowning.

I sat in the corner of the warehouse while a woman in all black barked orders at men taller than her by at least a foot. It seemed that the FBI was fighting with the local police.

Wasn't my problem.

I didn't give a shit.

Dimitri.

Quinn.

Who else was I going to lose?

Two ambulances came to take Marino and Quinn to the hospital. Marino was alive. Barely. If he lived, he'd stand trial. I hoped the bastard lived. I hoped he lived and spent the rest of his life in prison, locked away from the world, from any chance of rebuilding a life, from loving again.

Quinn…

They had to take her away and legally pronounce her dead.

"I was promised Aleksandr Drugov," the woman shouted, looking around, demanding someone answer her. "Where the fuck is Aleksandr Drugov?"

"Couldn't tell you," I snapped back. Now that Marino was indisposed, no doubt Drugov would come for my blood. But he wouldn't do it himself—he'd send one of his Russian assassins.

I wasn't concerned about that, though. Let them come. I would fight them. I'd fight them all, go to sleep, wake up, and do it all over again.

That would be my life.

"Where's Sean?" I asked softly.

Kilmartin stood next to me, like he was keeping watch. He looked down. "Not sure yet."

"So we don't even know if he's alive." I bent over and pressed my forehead to my knees. I wanted to get drunk and numb and never feel anything ever again. It had to be better than the pain that throbbed with every beat of my heart.

It had hurt me to leave Quinn, but I found a way to keep breathing.

Now that Quinn was gone, there was no reason to keep breathing. No reason to put one foot in front of the other. None of it mattered.

"Mr. Petrovich?" the woman said.

God, her voice was fucking abrasive.

"Mr. Petrovich."

"What?" I snapped, refusing to lift my head.

"Can we talk a moment? Alone?"

I looked up and met her eyes. Cool gray. "No. He stays."

When it was clear that I wouldn't stand, both Kilmartin and the woman sat on the ground. "I don't know if I introduced myself. Jordan Bennett."

"Archer's daughter," I said. "Right?"

She nodded, her delicate jaw clenching. She was rather attractive in a no nonsense, crush-your-balls-in-a-vice sort of way. Probably angry in bed.

When Quinn went to bed with me angry…

"What can I do for you?" I demanded. My tone was harsh, but I did nothing to reel it back.

"You promised me Aleksandr Drugov."

"I don't know where he is," I said. "He was supposed to be here."

She glared at me in frustration. "I realize that."

"Look, I don't have a lot of patience left, so let me give it to you straight. I've got nothing left to offer you. If Ori Marino lives, you can have him. Fight it out with the police." I looked at Kilmartin. "Why did the police come here, anyway? Your idea?"

"Quinn's," he said. His voice was raspy, like he'd been crying in private but refused to show the world his sadness. "Went to the Mayor. Marino's wanted for money laundering."

"Ori Marino is a small fish," Jordan stated. "I don't care about him."

"Spit it out, woman. What do you want from me?"

"Your help in getting Aleksandr Drugov. He's going to come after you, right?"

"I'd assume so."

I'd helped sell his daughter into slavery and now that Marino was no longer able to end my life, no doubt Drugov would pick up the sword.

"Great. Then you help me."

"Ask nicely," I said with a gruesome twist of my lips.

Her nostrils flared. "Please."

"Sure. Whatever. You have my cell. Now, can you leave me alone and let me fucking grieve in peace?"

"I'm sorry for your loss," she mumbled. Jordan got up and moved away, no doubt wanting to scream at someone else.

"She's terrifying," Kilmartin said. "I'm kind of in love with her."

I let out a gurgle of laughter, but it quickly turned into a choked sob. I shoved it down immediately. I would not break down. Not here. Not with witnesses.

"Want to get pissed?" Kilmartin asked. "After we find Sean, yeah?"

"Yeah."

"Come on, brother." He held out his hand to me. I grasped it and pulled myself up.

I wobbled and reached out to the wall to steady myself. "I don't know where to look for Sean."

"We should do a sweep of the area, just in case, though I doubt he's here."

"Yeah," I said in exhaustion. "God, what the fuck do I do if we find a body? I can't—I don't—" I closed my mouth, unable to get the words out.

The cell in my pocket vibrated. I pulled it out and looked at the number. New York area code. Didn't know it, but I answered it anyway.

"Hello?" I rasped.

"On a scale of one to ten," came Quinn's musical voice, "how was my performance?"

Chapter 46
SASHA

My heart leapt into my throat as I ran into the hospital. I hadn't even waited for Colleen to bring the car to a complete stop. I went to the desk and stumbled over Quinn's name, not sure what name she'd have been listed under.

The woman pressed a few buttons on her keyboard and then looked up at me and smiled. "Room eight eleven. Take these elevators and head to the west wing…"

I ran for the elevator. It seemed to take forever for it to arrive, and then it stopped on every floor. Finally, I got to the eighth floor and strode down the hall. When I came to room eight eleven, I stopped. I took in a deep breath and then opened the door.

She was sitting up in bed, her hands folded in her lap. Staring out the window, she didn't appear as if she'd heard me come in.

"Quinn," I whispered.

She turned her head and smiled. And then she laughed.

"It's not fucking funny," I snapped. Anger finally

pushed through the block of ice that had been my heart. It singed everything inside of me, setting it on fire. "Do you know—when I thought—"

"It's not funny," she agreed, her smile tripping. "But that's not why I'm laughing. It worked, Sasha. My plan worked."

"But your brother's life? You don't know if you—if your actions—"

"Impossible choices," she whispered.

I sat down on the hospital bed and stared at her. Her cheeks bloomed with color, and her green eyes sparkled with joy. I leaned over and kissed her like a man who'd gone off to war expecting to die, but who'd somehow made it home.

When I pulled away, she sank against me and pressed her hand to my heart. She didn't say anything for a long time. "What happened? To Ori?"

"No. You first. What happened from the moment you saw Marino at O'Malley Properties?"

She sat back and brushed the hair away from her cheeks. "We went to lunch. I asked for a divorce. He pretended to agree. Then he"—she touched the side of her neck—"did something. I don't know. Pressed a pressure point. The next thing I knew, I was in Glenmoore, strapped down." She inhaled a shaky breath. "You called Brandon?"

I nodded. "I trusted him to get you out."

"He's on the watched list. You know that, right?"

"I do."

"He came anyway," she murmured. "He got me out. Colleen came with him. You met his sister?"

I nodded again.

"They were going to try to take me to Belfast, but I— well, I grew a set and commandeered everything." She pressed her fingers to her lips. "I went to the Mayor. Old family friend, you know? I told him about what Ori was doing with my father's company."

"He sent the local police," I guessed.

"Yeah. They were going to prosecute Ori for money laundering. I was going to pretend to be the aggrieved unknowing wife. I wonder how the media will portray me," she added as an afterthought.

"We'll get there," I assured her. "Then what happened?"

"We got to New York—Brandon, Colleen, the Mayor, and me. I went to Chinatown…"

"You saw Lin," I said in realization.

She nodded. "Told him I was a friend of Barrett's and that I needed something to make it look like I was dead long enough to fool everyone—so that you could kill Ori." Her eyes were bright with anger. "Did you?"

I touched her cheek with my finger and trailed down her cheekbone. She shivered.

"No, Quinn. I didn't get a chance. The FBI was on us before that could happen."

"The FBI?" she asked in surprise. "What were they doing there?"

"I called them. Made a deal with Archer's trusted fellow. I promised her Aleksandr Drugov. But he wasn't there—Quinn, I don't know what happened to Sean. He might be—"

She put a hand to my mouth. "I know. Later." She dropped her hand and then laced her fingers through mine.

My gaze strayed to her belly. "The baby?"

"I—I'm still pregnant. But I won't know if I—"

I brought our clasped hands to my lips and bowed my head. "I'm so sorry, Quinn."

"For what?"

"For putting you in a position—where you had to choose between me or our—"

She cut me off with her lips. Her tongue swept inside my mouth, and before I knew it, she was on her back and cradling me in the vee of her thighs. I ached for her. Desperate and all-consuming. But here was not the place. Not in this sterile place where death constantly lingered.

Instead, I rolled onto my side and shared her bed, pulling her close to me. She snuggled against my side.

"You didn't even hesitate, did you?" she asked.

"Hmmm?" My fingers played with her hair, and my eyes closed.

"When they said they had my brother."

"No, I didn't hesitate." I thought about how I'd learned of Dimitri's death. Emotion clogged my throat when I thought of my friend, my trusted second. I wanted to tell Quinn about it, but I couldn't bear to give her any more loss. Not right now.

"What do we do?" she wondered.

I sighed. "Right now, we sleep."

Chapter 47
QUINN

I cracked an eyelid and saw that my room was full of people I didn't expect. Colleen was slumbering in a chair by the bed, Brandon was asleep propped up against a wall, and Barrett and Flynn were spooning on a cot.

Sitting up, I gently removed Sasha's arm from around me so I could climb out of bed. I tiptoed to the bathroom, wanting to make myself presentable.

When I'd gone to sleep, it had been nighttime, and only Sasha had been with me. The rest of them must've come during the middle of the night.

Everyone was stirring when I came back into the room. I wished I had my civilian clothes, but alas, I was stuck in yet another hospital gown.

Sasha rolled his shoulders and greeted everybody, not even seeming surprised. I couldn't say the same.

"What are you guys doing here?" I demanded.

"We were worried about you," Barrett said. She got up off the cot and came toward me. "Are you done in there? I've got to go."

"Me next," Colleen chimed in.

"A line for the ladies' room even at a hospital. Shocking," I drawled.

"Don't say anything until I get back, okay?" Barrett asked. "I want to hear everything."

"I only want to tell it once."

Brandon and Flynn left to get coffee for us. Sasha made me get back into bed, despite the fact that I was fine. Physically fine.

I worried about my brother. We hadn't been close in a long time, but I loved him. I didn't want anything bad to happen to him.

"Hey," Sasha whispered.

His soft smile drew my attention. We were together now. We'd figure everything else out…wouldn't we?

When everyone was back in the room, Sasha and I told them everything that had happened, each of us jumping in to fill in the gaps. It took the better part of an hour—and even I'd learned some new things.

"We lost Dimitri," Sasha said.

It hurt, deeply, to learn that the man was gone. He'd taken it upon himself to check up on me. He hadn't needed orders. He'd looked out for me because he was good.

"Shit," Flynn cursed.

"So, Ori's…" Barrett looked at me.

"In surgery, I guess." I glanced at Sasha. "I'm not sure."

He ran a hand across his face. Exhaustion was taking its toll. He'd lost weight, his eyes were dim, and no matter how much traction we seemed to gain, we always fell back. New blows, new landmines, new triggers. From all sides because we never saw them coming.

I cleared my throat and grasped Sasha's hand. "There

is one more thing that I think needs mentioning." Everyone quieted down and looked at me. "I'm pregnant. It's Ori's. But Sasha is—he will—"

"The child will never know its true biology. I've claimed him or her as my own."

"And no one outside this room will know otherwise." I pinned everyone with a stare.

It was so quiet it was deafening, like the sound of a city when it snowed. Barrett was the first to move. She jumped toward me and wrapped me in a tight embrace. Brandon and Flynn moved to shake Sasha's hand and pound him on the back.

Colleen hugged me next and whispered in my ear, "My brother will be very disappointed. He's always had a thing for you."

"Hush," I growled.

Her blue eyes twinkled when she pulled back.

We had a few moments of calm. I knew it wouldn't last. My brother was missing. Aleksandr Drugov was still out there determined to hunt down Sasha. And Ori was... If he lived, he'd stand trial. If he died, I'd be free.

"You really went to see Lin?" Barrett asked in amazement.

"Had to follow in your hallowed footsteps," I teased.

She waved her hand at me. "No need to follow in my steps, Quinn. You found your own way. You made it work how you needed to."

"You're just saying that."

"I'm not. You became a queen," she stated with a slight smile. "A queen fit for a king."

"Sure as hell beats being a princess."

Barrett laughed. "Right? Queens are badass. Princesses need protecting."

My eyes drifted to Sasha. He looked away from talking

with Flynn to stare at me. Everything I felt was reflected back in his eyes.

I had a man who'd give his life for mine. Just like I'd give my life for his. But what had I learned?

There was no life worth living without Sasha Petrovich.

Chapter 48

ORI

Twelve months later

Nonno took a seat across from me and rested his clasped hands on the table. He looked older in the year since I'd been put away. Speedy, public trial. Shame on my family. My dirty laundry brought to air. Soiled and stained with so much blood.

"Orange is a terrible color," Nonno said in Italian. "Why do they make you wear orange?"

I didn't reply. It wasn't worth one. Nonno was just warming up. He'd paid me a few visits over the last many months. Each time he looked more stooped, feeble, in danger of collapsing.

He was never supposed to have to fill this role again—not after I'd taken over.

I was a disgrace to the Marino name. A disgrace to the Abruzzo name.

I was tired. I had to be alert all the time. I had no friends. Allies, perhaps, but no friends. I was in a different league than the rest of the criminals who served their time next to me. It took energy to set things in motion—and from the inside—it was infinitely more difficult.

"Why did you come, Nonno?" I asked.

Nonno paused and then, "You have a daughter."

The fist around my heart eased just a bit. I'd known Quinn had lived. Taken something to make it look like she'd killed herself, killed my child in her womb. When I'd learned it had been a ploy, anger unlike anything I'd ever known had coursed through me. Not even the news of Igor's death had caused the same level of emotion.

"Did you hear me?" Nonno snapped.

"I heard you."

"The Russian bastard is raising her as his own. He's living with your wife—"

"She's not my wife," I interrupted. "It was annulled, remember?"

Nonno waved his hand. "You need to get your family back."

"What would you have me do? I'm in here. They're out there."

"You're a smart boy. Figure it out." His eyes glimmered with intelligence.

Even though we spoke in Italian—I refused to mention names. Names were dangerous.

"The other Russian?" I guessed.

Nonno smiled.

"He disappeared, no?"

"You find him. They bring him in. They let you go."

"Again, how am I supposed to do that when I'm in here?"

"You're a smart boy," he said again.

I hated when my grandfather spoke around me.

"I have other information," he said, changing the subject.

I raised an eyebrow and waited. Nonno liked to hear himself talk. He did not disappoint.

"It was not the Russian bastard who killed your friend."

Despite my desire to remain detached, I leaned forward. "What do you mean? He was the one who pulled the trigger."

Nonno shook his head. "No. There was another there. A woman."

"How do you know?" I asked with a frown. For years, I'd searched for someone who knew what had happened between Petrovich and Igor, but I never could find a lead.

Nonno looked smug. "You have to know who to ask."

Cryptic old bastard. "Keep your secrets, Nonno. Just tell me who was there."

He leaned closer and whispered a name.

I knew that name.

Petrovich's close friend.

Sitting back, a genuine smile crossed my lips. "Well, this just got interesting."

Chapter 49

ORI

I breathed in the fresh air as I buttoned my suit jacket. Glancing around, I saw the high fence of the security prison.

"Sir?" my driver said, holding the back door open for me.

I smiled. "Thank you." I climbed inside and breathed in the luxury around me. I'd missed this. Not that having bitches bring you cigarettes and warm your seat in the mess hall wasn't luxury, but I was accustomed to something else.

Turning in Drugov wasn't even a consideration. Not after what I'd learned. I couldn't get shit done the way I needed to from inside. I needed to be free.

Once I'd given Jordan Bennett the location of Drugov's hideout, it took only three weeks to get me out. I could've given Drugov up a year ago, but I hadn't wanted to be a snitch, hadn't wanted to look over my shoulder waiting for Drugov's men to come after me for betraying him. But this —the promise of freedom—to end Petrovich and the woman who killed Igor, was something I couldn't ignore.

I pressed the button to lift the divider between my driver and me. I reached into my pocket for my cell phone. Unlocking the screen, I stared at the photo.

Fucking gorgeous. Black hair, green eyes. I missed her in my bed. I missed her writhing beneath me.

I dialed her number, not expecting her to answer. Color me surprised when she did.

"Hello?" she asked, her voice low and raspy. Sexy as hell. I was hard immediately.

"Hey, *Cerbiatto*. You miss me?"

She inhaled sharply. "Ori?"

"Yeah, it's me."

"What are you—how did you—"

"I'm out."

"You're out." The words sounded like air from a deflating balloon. I could imagine her gripping the back of a chair and sinking to the floor. She was beautiful when she collapsed because I was strong enough to hold her up. She just didn't know it yet.

"I want to see you. And my daughter."

"You'll never see your daughter," she vowed. Her weak tone had grown in strength, surprising me again. What had she gained in the months I'd been gone? A spine? Had living with that Russian prick made her grow balls of steel?

"I'll see her," I said, pitching my voice low. "Or you'll never see your brother again."

She snorted. "You're bluffing. You have no idea where Sean is."

"No, *you* have no idea where your brother is. But I do."

"You're a liar and a sociopath. Like I'd believe anything you have to say."

"We'll be a family, Quinn. You, me, and the baby."

"I never loved you, Ori. It's always been Sasha. Everything I do, I do for Sasha. We'll be a family over my dead fucking body."

"No, Quinn. Over Sean's."

I hung up. Rage surged through my blood. Pulsing, hot and heavy. I didn't hesitate; I made another call, not caring about the time change.

"It's time. I want it there by breakfast." As I ended the call, I smiled. Quinn was about to learn who was in charge.

Chapter 50
QUINN

After Ori had survived surgery, after we'd discovered that Dimitri wasn't dead—just badly injured from a near fatal hit and run—Sasha and I had moved into a cottage on Martha's Vineyard.

We needed privacy after the backlash of the media. They hadn't painted me in a favorable light. Not that I cared. All I cared about was staying out of the public eye, tucked away and private.

I'd worried endlessly over the unknown fate of my brother. Months had passed without any word from him. I'd assumed him dead but refused to grieve for him until I knew. I hated that I'd gotten him wrapped up in this.

I hadn't even bothered tuning into the trial, just felt relief when Ori was sentenced.

But now?

Now he knew he had a daughter.

Now he wanted to see her.

Now he was coming for us again.

"Quinn?" Sasha called, closing the front door.

"In here," I said.

He came into the kitchen and stopped. "What's wrong? Is it Helena? Does she need—"

"Ori," I croaked. "Got out of prison."

His eyes narrowed. "How?"

"I don't know." I took a deep breath. "He wants to see her."

"Fuck no."

I nodded. "But he has Sean."

"How do you know?"

"I don't."

"He's a liar. A manipulator. You know this."

"I do. But I… I don't think he's lying."

"Fuck." He pinched the bridge of his nose.

A wail came through the baby monitor, and the both of us rushed from the kitchen to the nursery. Helena's tiny mouth was open in anger, her fists balled, ready to fight.

I scooped her up and brought her to the changing table. After she was dry, I sat down in the rocking chair and set her on my lap. I unbuttoned my blouse and then pressed her to my breast.

As she nursed, I rocked her, smoothing the dark hair on her head. But it wasn't dark like mine. It was chocolate brown—like Ori's. Another painful reminder that Sasha wasn't her biological father.

God bless him, he never looked at her like anything less.

His blue eyes softened when he gazed down at us.

"What do I do?" I whispered.

"You know," he said and pressed a kiss to my lips. "You know what to do."

"Another painful choice," I remarked. "Brother or daughter."

"More than that and you know it. It's your life, too. You know he won't stop. Not until he has you back."

"I knew he wasn't gone. But he was…out of sight. You know? Like I could pretend."

As my body had grown with Helena, Sasha whispered to her, sang to my belly Russian lullabies, promised her no man would ever be good enough.

He was her father—and blood didn't matter.

"I can't," my voice broke, "I can't sacrifice my child for my brother. It's—God, Sasha, if there is a hell, I know I'm going there."

"Stop," he commanded in such a forceful tone that Helena started to cry.

I instantly put her over my shoulder and patted her back, trying to soothe her and burp her at the same time. I breathed her in, that perfect baby smell that would one day all too soon disappear.

"You can't believe that, Quinn," he said, softening his tone. "You've done everything you can for those around you. The fact that Helena is with us, unharmed…"

I'd taken an uncalculated risk when I'd ingested the Chinese herbs, but the doctor had been able to detect a heartbeat, and we'd monitored her growth closely. She was born on time, with all her fingers and toes, no deficiencies. It's why I believed in God. And Hell. I didn't believe one existed without the other.

Not that I talked about it with others, but it was my own belief, and I held fast to it. If I sacrificed my brother for my child, did that make me the worst sort of person or just a mother?

I couldn't worry about that now. I only had to follow my heart, my instinct. And my instinct told me Ori Marino couldn't be rationalized with, and he'd take and take and take until there was nothing left.

"This was never supposed to be my life," I said softly.

Helena let out a magnificent burp and then snuggled into my neck. It was joy and pain.

"But it is. And wishing it were any other way is just naïve."

"You used to like that about me," I said to him with a winsome smile.

"But then you changed. And I like that too."

"We both changed," I said.

We fell silent and Sasha watched as I rocked the daughter of his heart to sleep.

The next morning, I woke up to a package from Ori Marino on my doorstep.

Inside was my brother's head.

Chapter 51
QUINN

I took a day. One full day to mourn my brother. It was time I couldn't afford to spare, but emotions didn't work on any sort of time clock. So I shoved them down and came out of the bedroom. As if being a sleep-deprived mother wasn't enough, I had to deal with the death of my brother and the reappearance of my sociopathic ex.

I entered the kitchen, head down, and went straight to the coffee.

"Quinn?" Sasha asked.

"I'm fine," I said, my voice hollow.

"No, you're not. Come here."

I set the coffee pot down and went to him. I let him pull me onto his lap. "Tell me what you want me to do. I'll do anything."

"I want him dead," I said, surprised at how calm my voice came out.

"But you—are you sure?"

"Yes. It won't stop otherwise. He won't stop."

Sasha's arms tightened around me.

"He wants me. He wants Helena. I can't let him, Sasha."

"Say it, Quinn. Ask me."

I looked him straight in the eye.

"Will you have Ori killed?"

He brushed hair away from my face and placed a kiss on my lips. A solemn vow. "*Da*."

Chapter 52

SASHA

I left Quinn and Helena to nap and headed down to the beach. It was private so it was quiet. It felt desolate, though, and I stared for a while at the cold, dark waves that crashed against the sand. Summer here had been bittersweet. Blue skies, cawing seagulls, walks along the surf, Quinn beautiful and round.

But our happiness always seemed to be tainted with the stain of destruction. And now the cycle continued. We'd come here to get away from all of it, but the reality was that it followed you. You couldn't outrun your past, and no matter how much you tried to bury it, it only took a few good storms to unearth the hidden pain you so wished to keep out of sight.

As afternoon turned to twilight, the sea air turned colder, and I lifted the collar of my coat to shield me from it. I picked my way back up to the house, a beautiful construction in the style of the island but completely modernized. It was supposed to be a safe haven, but it was rapidly becoming the place where more bad news found us.

I opened the front door and took off my shoes—Quinn hated sand in the house. I padded to the bedroom, not wishing to wake her up if she was still asleep. It was dark as I made my way to my side of the bed. Just as I got to the bedside, the light flared to life.

Quinn was sitting in a chair, her arms and legs bound. A gag was stuffed in her mouth, and her green eyes were wide with fear.

A man stood in the doorway, a gun trained at my head. He was only about five foot seven, nearly bald, carrying a bit of weight around the middle.

He smiled to reveal crooked teeth.

God, I hoped Helena didn't need braces.

I hoped I lived long enough to find out.

I rolled onto the bed and hit the ground just as the first bullet blew a hole in the wall behind where I'd been standing. Because I was me, because of who I was, I had weapons stashed all over the house, including a Glock under Quinn's side of the bed.

There was a magnet mount behind the headboard. I pulled out a Glock 19 and fired. The guy cursed, which meant I found my mark. But it wasn't fatal, and I hadn't taken him down.

I stood up, aimed for the guy's head, and fired.

Quinn screamed behind her gag as blood and brain matter coated her.

Helena cried, and I could hear her through the thick New England brick walls. I dropped the Glock on the bed and ran to Quinn. I quickly removed the gag, and then with the knife I carried on my belt, cut her loose.

"Helena," she whispered. Her hands shook as she gestured toward our daughter's room. I clasped them to me.

"I'll get her. You need to shower. Now."

"But I—"

"Quinn, shower."

She tried to look at the body on our bedroom floor, but I took her chin and diverted her gaze. Then I gave her a little push to the bathroom. Only when I heard the shower going did I turn, step over the prostrate form, and head to the nursery. On my way down the hall, I pulled out my phone and called one of my guys.

"Send the clean-up crew."

"Shit. Okay." He hung up.

A few of my men were on the island, staying close by. There was safety in numbers. Usually.

I got to Helena, but before I picked her up out of her crib, I stripped out of my shirt. Scooping her up, I began to sing a Russian lullaby to her, one my mother used to sing to my brother and me.

While I tended to my daughter, the front door opened and the boys came in. I ventured into the hallway and directed them to the bedroom. When they saw the destruction, they cursed.

"What the fuck?" Sergei demanded. "Marino?"

I shrugged. "Probably, but I don't know for sure. The assassin wasn't very chatty."

"Where's Quinn?"

"In the bathroom. She should be there for a while." I sighed and then told him what had happened.

"Seriously?" He shook his head. "You keep me busy." Sergei looked down at Helena who was hiccoughing against my T-shirt.

He smiled at her and gently stroked her cheek. "We'll get this straightened up."

I took the baby and sat down on the couch. Stretching out my long legs, I leaned back and searched for my phone. I called Barrett, but she didn't answer.

EMMA SLATE

When it rolled to voicemail I hung up and dialed her husband. He answered on the first ring.

"Someone just tried to kill me," I said.

"No shite."

"I called Barrett, but she didn't answer."

"Girls' night," he said.

"Flynn."

He paused. "You called me by my first name."

"Check on her," I said, pitching my voice low. "Barrett always answers when I call."

"Not always," he growled. "Not when I'm inside her—"

"Don't have time for this." I kept my voice low, so I didn't startle Helena who had just started to settle. "You know what I mean."

He sighed. "All right."

"Call me back," I stated.

"I will."

I set my phone aside and stroked Helena's back, trying not to let the worry get the best of me. But when Campbell didn't call back, I knew something was wrong.

Chapter 53

QUINN

I threw up in the shower.

I washed my hair three times and scrubbed my skin until it was nearly raw. The water was as hot as I could stand, and still it wasn't hot enough.

Finally, drained of energy and the contents of my stomach, I climbed out of the shower. I wrapped the towel around me and opened the bathroom door. A billow of steam poured out, but when it cleared, I saw three men in my bedroom ripping up the stained carpet.

The body was gone as were the remains of him on the furniture and the walls.

I was almost sick again.

"Hey, Quinn," Sergei said.

The men diverted their eyes, but I still wished I were in something more than a towel. I quickly gathered a spare change of clothes and then went into the bathroom again. After I towel dried my hair, I combed it and then went to find Sasha.

He was on the couch, and Helena was sleeping on top of him.

"Do you want her?" he asked quietly.

I shook my head. "She's comfortable." I leaned back in the chair and pinched the bridge of my nose.

"Headache?"

"A little one." We fell silent for a moment, and then I spoke. "This was all Ori."

"Probably."

"Do you think…do you think that man was going to kill me? After he killed you?"

Sasha took a moment to reply, and then finally he shook his head. "If he wanted you dead, why did he wait? You were alone. I left you alone."

"No, no guilt."

He gave me a watery smile, but it dimmed. "No. He wanted you to watch me die."

"I thought you…" I looked behind me toward the direction of the bedroom but none of Sasha's men were around. Still, I pitched my voice lower. "I thought you were taking care of it?"

"I am taking care of it," he growled. "But it's not as simple as making a phone call and transferring money. My guy is in—no, never mind. You're never going to know. I don't want you to know."

"I don't want to know," I muttered. "I just want it done. So this doesn't happen again."

"Ori wanted me to die in front of you," he said. "He wanted it bloody and painful for you. Just like what he did with your brother."

I swallowed.

"We're done here," Sergei said, coming into the living room. The two guys behind him carried the rolled-up rug out the front door. "Sorry about this, Quinn." And then he disappeared too.

Once the door closed and we were left in privacy, Sasha said, "You need to call him."

"What?" I gasped.

"The assassin didn't have a cell phone on him. You have to call Marino and tell him his guy got the job done and I'm dead, or Marino will know he didn't succeed. You want this over with? You want this done now? Then Marino needs to think you're open and vulnerable. He needs to think you're ripe for the picking."

"I'm a shitty liar," I stated. "I can't lie to save my life. He'll know that."

"You seemed to do okay in the warehouse," he reminded me.

My eyes fell from his.

"Look at our daughter," he said, his tone soft yet forceful. "If you don't do this, he wins. He'll take her from you. Are you going to let that happen?"

I stood up slowly and strode toward the bedroom. The once warm room now looked barren and cold. I closed the door and went to my side of the bed and forced myself to stare at the spot on the wall that had been cleaned.

My phone rested on my bedside table. I unlocked it and then scrolled to the only recent number in my call log. With a deep breath, I pressed it.

My heart trumpeted as I waited for him to pick up. I didn't give him a chance to utter an Italian endearment.

"You fucking bastard," I croaked. I sounded like I'd been crying. I had been, maybe. On the inside. "Enough, Ori. Enough." I finally broke down and started to sob, and there was nothing fabricated about it.

"Quinn." He said my name soft and gentle.

"You took the rest of them from me," I whispered. "I've got nothing left."

"You've got me. You've got our daughter."

"You win, then. Congratulations," I said, my tone bitter yet defeated.

"I'll be there in a few hours."

Chapter 54
QUINN

I sat on the couch with only the lamps on. It was strangely romantic, and I forced myself not to think about all the nights in this room with Sasha, with his fingers drawing swirls on my belly.

The front door opened. I didn't turn because I knew who was there. Ori had a presence. A dark malevolence he brought, along with the winter wind.

His footsteps were quiet across the living room floor. He came around and sank down on the couch next to me. Ori reached out to gently grasp my chin and turned my face toward him. He leaned in to brush his lips against mine.

"I've missed you, *Cerbiatto*." He ran his hand down my hair. "It's longer. I like it."

Still, I said nothing.

"Your bags are packed?"

I nodded.

"And Helena's?"

I nodded again.

"Where is she?" he demanded.

"Sleeping. In the nursery."

"I've never seen her," he murmured, as if I wasn't there.

"I never wanted you to."

He frowned. "Please. Not tonight, Quinn."

I shrugged, as if I couldn't care less.

"I'd like to…hold her."

"Go ahead," I said. "Not like I can stop you."

Ori sighed but said nothing. He got up off the couch and strode toward the hallway, past the bedroom.

"Huh," he said.

"What?" I asked, turning my head.

He appeared back in the living room. "Your bedroom…it looks..."

My heartbeat tripped. "It happened in there. I had Sasha's men come. I couldn't stand to see him…"

Ori stared at me for a long moment, and I refused to flinch or divert my eyes. I let him see my sadness, my grief.

With a nod, he headed toward the nursery. I heard the door squeak open and then the music playing from the mobile. The sound was supposed to cover any white noise in the room, so Ori wouldn't hear Sasha coming at him from behind.

But Ori was no fool, and I knew he had to be carrying.

I wondered what would happen when he realized Helena wasn't in her crib. She was with our neighbors over the hill, safe and warm. Far away from Ori's clutches.

There was a scuffle and then a few popping noises.

A moment later, Sasha came into the living room and took the seat next to me. He wrapped his arm around me and pulled me close.

"It's done," he said quietly, pressing his lips to my forehead.

"Done," I repeated. "And you're okay? He didn't get—"

"No. We're safe now."

I leaned up to kiss him. "Thank you." It didn't feel real. Not yet. Ori was gone… and I wasn't sure how to reconcile my feelings.

"Let's go get Helena."

His thumb stroked the apple of my cheek, and then he kissed the end of my nose. "In a minute. I need to call Campbell and let him know." He pulled out his phone from his pocket and turned it on. His screen pinged with dozens of missed calls and texts.

"What's going on?" I asked.

"I don't know. Hold on." He pressed a button. "Campbell? Yeah. It's done. We—What? She's where?" He closed his eyes. "All right. We're on the first flight out."

"What's wrong?" I asked when he hung up.

"Barrett." His face was grim. "She's in the hospital."

Chapter 55
QUINN

"Stop fussing over me," Barrett groused as Flynn fluffed her pillow.

"You're my wife. You were shot. You almost died. *Again*. It's my right to fuss. Now shut up and let me be your sexy Scottish nurse."

She pretended to look affronted, but she caught my eye and winked.

I laughed which woke up Helena.

"The best cure for a gunshot wound to the belly is holding a baby. Gimme." She held out her arms, and I gently placed Helena into the cradle of them.

"Easy," Flynn said. "You don't have your strength back."

She snorted and clearly didn't listen to him.

"Your wife is incredibly resilient," Sasha remarked dryly.

"As is your—uh—what is Quinn to you?" Flynn asked, pitching us both a look.

"You're such a busybody," Barrett said. "They'll get married when they get married. Leave them alone."

"They've been living together for a year. They're raising a baby together. It's time for them to—"

"Hey, guys," I voiced. "Mind if we have a say in the matter about the state of our relationship?"

"I guess," Barrett said. "Okay. I'm kicking the boys out. I need to talk to Quinn."

"Come on." Flynn slapped Sasha on the back. "Let me buy you a drink."

"It's ten o'clock in the morning," Sasha mused.

"So?"

"Yeah, you're right. Let's go."

The door to the hospital room closed, and I sat down in the chair next to the bed, ready for the inquisition.

"How are you doing?" Barrett asked without taking her eyes off my daughter.

"I should be asking you that."

"It's been three days. I'm almost ready to run a marathon."

"Seriously, Barrett."

"It hurts, but I'm not dying of sepsis or organ failure. Now you."

"Am I terrible for saying I'm relieved?"

"No. He made your life hell."

"He did. Yes."

"Still, you did get something beautiful out of it." She looked at me and smiled gently.

I gazed at Helena, content in Barrett's arms. "I wasn't sure we'd be able to pull it off. I thought Ori would realize it was a trap."

"The man was desperate enough to come for you. Come for you and Helena."

"Apparently. I guess he really believed I had no one left and that we could truly be a family." I shook my head. "My brother…"

"Flynn told me Marino used his family's restaurant insurance money to hire the hit on Sean."

I nodded and took a moment to think of my brother. How scared he must've been. I sent up a silent prayer that he found peace.

"Igor didn't see clearly. In the end. Hubris, I think."

"Yes. Probably had been Ori's downfall too."

We both fell silent, lost in our own thoughts.

"Now I feel like I can grieve, you know?" I said, ready to talk again. "All the things I've had to shove aside. Grieve and face forward."

"You'll get there," she assured me. "Take her back. My arms are tired."

"I thought you said you could—"

"I lied. I hate when Flynn thinks he's right. He's arrogant on a normal day. I don't need him lording it over me now."

I laughed and took Helena back into my arms. She snuggled against me and fell asleep. I didn't think I'd ever get tired of that.

"Treasure those moments," Barrett said, obviously knowing what I was thinking. "They'll be gone before you know it. Then she'll be a child who asks questions like *Mam, why are ye in a hospital. Again?*"

"Hey, your brogue sounds pretty good," I teased. I looked down at Helena's innocent face. "Part of me thinks he left the best part of himself with me. Is that stupid?"

"No. That's motherhood."

Chapter 56
QUINN

Another three days later, and Barrett was home from the hospital. The house was filled with flowers of all species and colors. Duncan and Ash, with their children, were there to greet her. Not to mention, the Campbell boys who were as rowdy as ever. Betty the sheep had her special place near Barrett's feet or on her lap, much to Flynn's aggravation.

"It always smells like wet wool in this house," he groused.

"It does not, you old grump."

"Old? Who you calling old?" he demanded with a blistering frown at his wife.

She smiled up at him. "You're not old? Prove it."

He leaned down and whispered something in her ear that caused her to laugh.

"Stop it," Ash and I said at the same time, producing another round of laughter.

It felt good to laugh and to be surrounded by family and children. It was a life I never thought I'd get to live.

I looked at Sasha who blatantly ignored the Campbells' devoted, passionate looks to each other.

He leaned over and gently pressed a kiss to my lips.

Once others saw us kissing, we were the center of attention. The marriage questions kept coming. I thought about answering, but Sasha squeezed my hand and shook his head.

We'd talked about it enough. About how marriage didn't prove anything to us. I'd been married, and it had been a cage. It wasn't about the piece of paper or having the same last name. Not for us.

I was Quinn O'Malley.

He was Sasha Petrovich.

And there was nothing more to say about it.

The next morning, all the adults congregated around the dining room table for breakfast, while the herd of nannies took care of the even bigger herd of children.

"If Helena needs you, they'll let you know," Sasha said, pulling me into his side. "Let's enjoy some adult conversation, huh?"

I kissed his lips, feeling a little sleepy. Sasha had kept me awake late last night making love to me by the light of the Scottish moon. There was something magical about Scotland.

He held my chair for me. When the six of us were all seated, food began to appear before us. Scones, eggs, bacon, toast, muffins. Everything we could ever want. A true feast, a celebration.

"Got a call from Jordan Bennett this morning," Flynn said as he reached for his glass of freshly squeezed orange juice.

"Jesus, why?" Duncan asked. "The woman is terrifying."

Ash elbowed him. "You've never even met her."

"I've heard enough about her to be terrified." The big, burly Scotsman pretended to shiver in fear.

We all laughed, as was his intent.

"As I was saying," Flynn went on, like he hadn't been interrupted. "She called. Seems Aleksandr Drugov died in prison while waiting for his trial."

No one said anything for a moment, and then Ash voiced, "Pity."

"Crying shame," Duncan agreed.

"Okay, confess," Flynn demanded with a look at Sasha.

Sasha shook his head. "Wasn't me."

Flynn glanced at me.

"Seriously?" I demanded. "Yeah, right."

The man slowly swiveled his head to stare at his wife who was looking at the butter dish. "You guys have to try this butter. It's from Moira—"

"Barrett," Flynn growled.

She sighed. "You guys were kind of occupied—with a lot of stuff." She peered at her husband. "You had the Waco business." She turned her gaze to me. "And you had the Marino business. So, I took it upon myself and hired the—"

"Enough," Flynn stated. "That's enough. We got it."

We all focused on our plates and went back to eating. Only when I caught Barrett's eye, I started to giggle. And then she started to giggle. And then Ash started to giggle. Soon we were a giggling mess while three men looked at us like we were certifiable. Maybe we were. Talking about hiring hits and Irish butter in the same sentence.

Just a normal breakfast for this mafia family

Sasha's hand reached for mine under the table.

I gave it a squeeze.

I wouldn't trade it for anything.

Chapter 57
QUINN

I entered the guest bedroom, and my heart swelled. The bedside lamp was on. Half of Sasha's face was in shadow, the side that hadn't been touched by fire. His eyes were closed, and his hand was on Helena's back. Her head was turned away, so all I saw was her tiny little ear, pink in the lamp glow.

They were a perfect picture, and I took a moment to watch them.

Sasha stirred and opened his eyes. He grinned sleepily at me. "Hi," he said. His voice was low and raspy. Quiet, so he wouldn't disturb her.

"Hi," I said with a smile. I went to the bed and sat down next to him. I leaned over and brushed my lips across his. "Let me take her."

I reached down and picked her up. She was a heavy sleeper, so she didn't stir as I placed her in the bassinet.

"Did you have a good time with Barrett?" he asked.
"Yes."

I turned back and stared down at him as my hands went to the buttons of my shirt. I kept my gaze on him as I slowly removed my clothes. And then I straddled him, naked and wanting.

"Quinn," he whispered as his hand came to the back of my head to pull my mouth to his.

He kissed me with languid patience, stroking the flames of desire. But it took no time before I was begging for him, begging for his body on top of mine.

Sasha gently rolled me off him so my back was against the covers. He quickly stripped out of his clothes.

I wanted my hands to be everywhere. I wanted to trace his scars with my lips. I wanted him to know he was beautiful.

"You're perfect," he growled.

I smiled. "I was thinking the same thing about you."

He eased inside of me, filling me. "I love you "

"I know."

Sasha started to move, and I closed my eyes, enjoying the feel of him. Skin to skin. No barriers. No hiding.

I came quickly and quietly.

With a few more thrusts, Sasha found his release and collapsed on top of me.

We held each other while the Scottish storm beat relentlessly against the windows. Lightning and thunder. Gray and dark.

But eventually we slept.

And Sasha made love to me in the dawn of the new day, and when our daughter cried, he got up to bring her to bed.

I put her to my breast, and while she nursed, I looked up at the man I loved more than life itself.

"Marry me," he said quietly, his blue eyes intense and hopeful. His hand reached out to stroke my hair. "Please, Quinn."

I leaned up and pressed a smiling kiss to his lips. "All right, Sasha. All right."

Additional Works

The Tarnished Angels Motorcycle Club Series:

Wreck & Ruin (Book 1)
Crash & Carnage (Book 2)
Madness & Mayhem (Book 3)
Thrust & Throttle (Book 4)
Venom & Vengeance (Book 5)
Fire & Frenzy (Book 6)
Leather & Lies (Book 7)
Heartbeats & Highways (Book 8 - preorder)

SINS Series:

Sins of a King (Book 1)
Birth of a Queen (Book 2)
Rise of a Dynasty (Book 3)
Dawn of an Empire (Book 4)
Ember (Book 5)
Burn (Book 6)

Ashes (Book 7)
Fall of a Kingdom (Book 8)

Others:

Peasants and Kings

About the Author

Wall Street Journal & USA Today bestselling author Emma Slate writes romance with heart and heat.

Called "the dialogue queen" by her college playwriting professor, Emma writes love stories that range from romance-for-your-pants to action-flicks-for-chicks.

When she isn't writing, she's usually curled up under a heating blanket with a steamy romance novel and her two beagles—unless her outdoorsy husband can convince her to go on a hike.

.

www.ingramcontent.com/pod-product-compliance
Lightning Source LLC
Chambersburg PA
CBHW031442200726
48289CB00007BB/2137